DEATH OF A SWEEP

A Hamish Macbeth Murder Mystery

M. C. Beaton

Constable • London

CONSTABLE

First published in the USA by Grand Central Publishing,
a division of Hachette Book Group USA, Inc., 2011

First published in Great Britain in 2011 by Robinson,
an imprint of Constable & Robinson

This edition published in 2013 by Constable

3 5 7 9 10 8 6 4

A CIP catalogue record for this book
is available from the British Library.

ISBN: 978-1-47210-545-5

Printed and bound in Great Britain by
CPI Group (UK) Ltd, Croydon CR0 4YY

Papers used by Constable are from well-managed forests and
other responsible sources

MIX
Paper from
responsible sources
FSC® C104740
www.fsc.org

Constable
An imprint of
Little, Brown Book Group
Carmelite House
50 Victoria Embankment
London EC4Y 0DZ

An Hachette UK Company
www.hachette.co.uk

www.littlebrown.com

To Georgie Askew and Dave Tapping and to the staff of the beautiful Cavendish Hotel on the Chatsworth Estate who sheltered us one whole winter's afternoon, although we were not guests. Many thanks.

And Hamish Macbeth fans
share their reviews . . .

'Treat yourself to an adventure in the Highlands;
remember your coffee and scones – for you'll want
to stay a while!'

'I do believe I am in love with Hamish.'

'M. C. Beaton's stories are absolutely excellent . . .
Hamish is a pure delight!'

'A highly entertaining read that will have me
hunting out the others in the series.'

'Once I read the first mystery I was hooked . . . I
love her characters.'

Share your own reviews and comments at
www.constablerobinson.com

Chapter One

Golden lads and girls all must,
As chimney-sweepers, come to dust.
— WILLIAM SHAKESPEARE

The village of Drim in the county of Sutherland in the north-west of Scotland was rarely visited by outsiders. Not even the most romantic member of the tartan lunatic fringe of the lowland cities could claim it to be a place of either interest or beauty.

It was a small village situated at the end of the long arm of a sea loch where towering mountains dropped down sheer into the water so that the loch looked black and sinister even on a fine day. It consisted of a huddle of white-washed cottages and one general store. There had been a murder committed there some time ago, temporarily bringing in the outside world, but since then Drim had settled back into its usual torpor.

There was no longer a resident minister, although the church was served every three

1

Sundays by a visiting preacher. The old manse stood empty, and no one showed any signs of buying it. Furthermore, it was said to be haunted because the last minister had hanged himself after his wife had run off and left him.

The nearest policeman, Police Sergeant Hamish Macbeth, was some miles away across mountain and moorland in the village of Lochdubh, and although Drim was on his beat, he rarely had any reason to visit the place.

There was, however, a brief burst of excitement when newcomers bought an old Georgian mansion up on the brae above the village. It had lain empty for some time, the previous owner having been an eccentric old lady. The house had been on the market for five years before it was bought by a Captain Henry Davenport and his wife, Milly.

It was a square three-storeyed building in red sandstone, as unprepossessing and as grim as the village. It would have commanded a good view of the surrounding landscape had not the house been ringed by laurels, Douglas firs, stands of birch, and one giant monkey puzzle.

A few of the villagers had called on the English couple when they first moved in four months before with presents of cake but were repelled by the pompous manner of the captain and the faded timidity of his wife. They drove down to the nearest town, Strathbane, to

2

do all their shopping, and so Milly Davenport did not even visit the local store.

Captain Henry Davenport had retired from the Army, slightly bitter at not having risen higher in the ranks, but determined still to be addressed by his military title. Nowhere else in the country could he have afforded to buy such a large house, and it suited his grandiose ideas.

Milly, his wife, also English, still showed signs of having once been pretty. She would have liked to employ one of the women in the village to help her with the cleaning, but her husband said acidly that she had nothing else to do with her time and it would be a waste of money.

The captain had discovered that a peat bank belonged to the house, and so he employed a local man, Hugh Mackenzie, to keep him supplied with peat. But the fire smoked dreadfully. One evening, the captain received a rare phone call. He came back from the phone, which was still located in the draughty hall where it had stood since the days when it was first installed, his face flushed and worried.

'Who was on the phone, dear?' asked Milly.

'Just an old Army friend. Look, do something useful. I'm going out for a walk tomorrow. Get some exercise. Get the sweep in and get the damn chimney cleaned! If anyone calls, tell them I've gone abroad.'

* * *

3

In less remote parts of Scotland, people had their chimneys vacuum-cleaned. But in Drim, villagers relied on the services of the itinerant sweep, Pete Ray, with his old-fashioned brushes.

Chimney sweeps are still regarded as lucky at weddings, especially if they kiss the bride. Pete made extra money from being hired to kiss brides even though people swore he had only two baths a year: one at Christmas and the other at Easter. Mostly he was as black as the soot he took from the chimneys. He lived in a hut high up on the moors between Lochdubh and Drim. He drove an old-fashioned motorcycle with a sidecar to carry his brushes.

Milly obtained his phone number by calling the local store. Just before he arrived, the captain said mysteriously that he planned to be out for some time and repeated that if anyone asked for him, she should say he had gone abroad.

The sweep arrived just after the captain had left. Milly took one look at his soot-covered appearance, gave him a mug of tea, and then rushed to spread newspapers and old sheets over the drawing-room carpet. She then said she was going to walk down to the village to get some groceries. She asked Pete how much it would cost and then gave him the money, saying if she was not back by the time he had finished, to leave by the kitchen door, lock the

4

door behind him, and put the key through the letter box. She had a spare key. Milly was determined to be out of the house for as long as possible in case whoever it was her husband wanted to avoid should come calling. Milly knew herself to be incapable of lying without giving herself away.

Also, she had had little chance of meeting any of the women from the village and was longing to talk to someone, anyone, who was not her husband. She spent very little in the local shop, knowing that her husband took a malicious delight in not giving the locals any custom, but she chatted to several of the women and a Mrs Mackay invited her back for tea.

Happy for the first time in ages, Milly returned home after several hours. She was annoyed to find the kitchen door standing open, and then assumed that either the sweep had forgotten to lock it or her husband had come back. Milly picked up the sheets from the floor and put them in the laundry room. There were still crumpled newspapers in the hearth where she had left them to catch any fall of soot. She decided to have a glass of whisky before she did any more cleaning. She took one of her husband's precious bottles of malt whisky from the sideboard and poured herself a generous measure. Her husband would not approve, but he was often so drunk in the evenings that she was sure he would assume he had drunk the whisky himself.

She sat down in the drawing room, sipping her drink and staring at the large stone fireplace. She had enjoyed her little bit of freedom. If only her husband would go away more often! *If only*, whispered a nasty little voice in her head, *he were dead*.

Feeling guilty, Milly took another sip of her drink, listening all the while for her husband's return. The wind had got up and was blowing around the house.

Plop! Plop! Plop! Milly stiffened. What was that noise? A leaky tap in the kitchen? No, the noise seemed to be coming from the fireplace. Darkness was falling. She got up and switched on all the lights.

Plop!

The noise was coming from the fireplace. She walked over to it and stared. Something dark was falling in drips on to the paper. The chimney was old. If you bent down and looked up it, you could see the sky. Perhaps it was rain.

She caught a drop on the back of her hand and then held her hand under a lamp on a table by the fireside.

Milly let out a whimper of fear. Blood!

By the time Police Sergeant Hamish Macbeth arrived from Lochdubh, Milly had shut herself in the kitchen. 'It's blood dripping down the chimney,' she cried when she opened the door to the tall policeman.

'Now, then,' said Hamish soothingly. 'It may be a bird or animal stuck up there.'

'But the sweep was here and cleaned the chimney.'

'When was that?'

'This morning.'

'And where is your husband?'

'He went out for a walk. He's not back yet.'

'In the drawing room, you said?'

'Yes, let me show you.' Milly led the way. The drawing room was sparsely furnished with Swedish assemble-it-yourself furniture, unsuited to what had once been an elegant room.

Hamish took out a powerful torch, crouched down, and shone it up the chimney. The torchlight fell on a dangling pair of highly polished brogues.

He sat back on his heels. 'I'm afraid there's a body stuck in the chimney.'

'Oh, that poor sweep!' gasped Milly.

Hamish did not like to tell her that Pete had never worn anything on his feet but dirty, cracked old boots. He telephoned police headquarters and demanded the lot – ambulance, fire department, Scenes of Crime Operatives, and police.

He turned to Milly and said gently, 'Chust

you be going ben to the kitchen. This iss not the place for you.'

While he waited, Hamish fretted. What if the man up the chimney was not dead? But if he pulled the body down, he would be accused of having ruined a possible crime scene.

To his relief, he heard the wail of sirens approaching. Hamish stood back to let the white-suited SOCO men into the room first and then went into the kitchen to join Detective Chief Inspector Blair, a thickset Glaswegian who hated him, and Blair's side-kick, Jimmy Anderson.

Hamish reported what he had found. 'I think it's Captain Davenport,' he said. 'And we'd better find that sweep.'

'Then get to it,' snapped Blair, 'and leave this to the experts.'

There was a short drive at the front of the house, shadowed by trees and bushes. Tyre marks in the gravel showed that the sweep had ridden round to the kitchen door at the side.

Hamish went to the general store first where Jock Kennedy and his wife, Ailsa, served behind the counter. He told them what had happened and then appealed to Ailsa, 'I think Mrs Davenport could do wi' a bit of female company.'

'I'll get up there right away,' said Ailsa.

Hamish then headed up over the moors to the hut in which Pete Ray lived. He knocked, but there was no reply. He walked around the hut amongst bits of old rusting machinery but could not see the motorbike. He tried the door of the hut and found it unlocked. He entered, flashing his torch this way and that because he knew the hut did not have any electricity. It consisted of one room with a Calor-gas stove in one corner, a dirty unmade bed against one wall, an old iron stove, and a jumble of magazines heaped on the floor beside the bed. A curtained recess contained one good suit and, lying underneath the suit on the floor, a heap of underwear and dirty sweaters.

He went back outside, experiencing a feeling of dread. He could not see Pete committing such a pointless and elaborate murder. Hamish took out his phone and called Jimmy Anderson. 'Can't see Pete anywhere,' he said.

'Blair's got an all-points out on him,' said Jimmy, 'although I don't see how a sweep on an old-fashioned bike should suddenly become invisible.'

'I can,' said Hamish gloomily.

'What?'

'What if the murderer was interrupted by the sweep, killed him, drove his bike off to the nearest peat bog, and made the lot disappear?'

'Trust you to go complicating things.'

* * *

9

But the next day, Pete was found dead up on the moors. It appeared his motorcycle had struck a hollow hidden in the heather and had catapulted him on to a sharp rock. His neck was broken. He was clutching a tyre iron matted with hair and blood. In the sidecar were found silver candlesticks, the captain's wallet, and Milly's jewellery. Case closed. Pete had been caught by the captain and had killed him.

The following evening when Jimmy called at the police station in Lochdubh, he found Hamish Macbeth in a truculent mood.

'I dinnae believe it,' exclaimed Hamish. 'Not Pete. He was a gentle soul and he loved his chimneys. He was a bit simple in a way. But vicious? Neffer!'

'Oh, calm down and give me a dram,' said Jimmy.

Hamish poured him a measure of whisky. 'It's like this,' he said. 'Davenport tells the wife that he is going out for a walk and if anyone asks for him to say he's gone abroad.'

'You've been hacking into the police computers again,' accused Jimmy.

Hamish ignored that remark and went on: 'So say this person meets him and they walk back to the house. This person quarrels with Davenport and bashes his head in wi' a tyre iron, and then like a bad elf, down the chimney, out pops Pete. It's one of thae old-fashioned chimneys with climbing rungs inside from the days when the sweep sent a boy up. Pete could get up there himself. He was all skin and bone. The murderer kills him, takes a few objects to make it look as if Pete was a robber as well, gets him in the sidecar, and goes off over the moors to fake the whole thing. Returns to the house and searches for something he wants, can't find it, and in a rage he stuffs the captain up the chimney, the captain himself being pretty skinny, hoping it'll be some time before the body is found.'

'Oh, come on, Hamish. Let it go.'

'No! I bet forensics never examined that sidecar properly. I want to see it.'

'It's eight o'clock, laddie.'

'Come on, Jimmy. Let's go.'

'All right. Leave your beasts behind. They give me the shivers.'

Hamish's 'beasts' were a dog called Lugs and a wild cat called Sonsie. Jimmy should have known that Hamish would no more consider leaving them behind than he would a pair of small children.

Hamish set off driving his Land Rover while Jimmy followed in his unmarked police car.

There was a mildness in the evening air as if winter were at last releasing its grip on Sutherland. Great stars blazed above, with the towering mountains black silhouettes against the bright sky.

* * *

11

The head of SOCO was a beefy, fierce man called Angus Forrest. 'I'm packing up for the night,' he growled.

'We just want a wee look at that sweep's sidecar,' said Jimmy.

'I was going to go over it tomorrow. Doesn't seem much point. Open-and-shut case.'

'Won't take us long,' said Jimmy stubbornly. The motorcycle and sidecar were parked in a garage at the side of police headquarters. Angus switched on the overhead lights. 'I'm off to the pub,' he said. 'Phone me when you've finished. But suit up and get your gloves on.'

Jimmy and Hamish struggled into their blue forensic suits and boots. 'Now,' said Hamish, his hazel eyes gleaming, 'let's see what we can find. I suppose the tyre iron and the jewellery and wallet have all been bagged up, but it's that sidecar that interests me. We need luminol.'

'What do you think this is?' grumbled Jimmy. 'The telly? Got a fingerprint kit?'

'Got it with me.'

'Okay, dust away. I'll sit over there and watch you.'

Hamish carefully began to dust the sidecar and motorbike. He finally straightened up. 'Whoever drove this wore gloves. When did Pete wear gloves?'

'When he'd just murdered someone,' said Jimmy, stifling a yawn.

'But there are no fingerprints, and the side-car has been wiped clean.'

'Pete's fingerprints were found on the candlestick and on the captain's wallet.'

'Aye, you can press a dead man's hand on the stuff. I need a damp cloth.'

'What for?'

'Never mind. I'll use my handkerchief.' Hamish ran it under a tap and wrung it out. Then he bent into the sidecar and gently dabbed at the floor.

He straightened up. 'There's blood on the floor.'

'Aye, well, laddie, there would be. The captain's blood.'

'What is going on here?'

Superintendent Daviot appeared in the doorway. 'Macbeth, you are not a member of SOCO or forensics. How dare you tamper with evidence?'

'Sir,' said Hamish, 'there's blood in the sidecar, and I think you'll find it belongs to Pete.'

'What are you trying to tell me?'

Once more, Hamish expounded his theory.

'I want you to get out of here and leave it to the experts,' snapped Daviot.

'I don't think they were even going to bother,' said Hamish. 'It's dangerous to let the real murderer go free.'

'Are you trying to tell me how to do my job?'

Hamish raised his hands. 'A brilliant man like yourself? Oh, no, sir, wasn't I chust saying

13

to Jimmy that a brain like Superintendent Daviot's could never be fooled by faked evidence.'

Daviot shifted uneasily. He considered Hamish Macbeth a maverick but one who had an awkward way of getting things right.

'Phone Forrest and get him back here,' he said.

When Angus appeared, he was ordered to take samples of the blood from the sidecar and get the DNA checked as soon as possible. 'And check those fingerprints on the wallet,' said Hamish eagerly, 'and see if they look genuine or if a dead man's hand could have been used to make the marks.'

'See to it,' said Daviot. 'On your way, Macbeth. Anderson, I want a word with you.'

As Hamish left, he could hear Angus's protesting voice raised in anger. He looked at his watch. It was too late to call on Milly Davenport. He would go and see her in the morning. Why had the captain left his wallet behind? Or had it been taken from his body?

But on the following morning, Hamish received a call summoning him to police head-quarters. On his arrival in Daviot's office, he was told he was suspended pending inquiries into his unorthodox behaviour by investigating a crime scene when he did not have the necessary forensic skills.

'You are so anxious to close the case, sir,'

14

said Hamish angrily, 'that nothing would have been properly inspected.'

'Don't be insolent and get out of here before I fire you,' said Daviot.

Hamish met Jimmy Anderson on his way out. 'I hope I didn't get you into trouble, Jimmy.'

'Not me. I know how to grovel and crawl when necessary.'

'Do you think they won't bother with the DNA?'

'Oh, they'll bother all right. Blair's rubbing his fat hands and demanding a rush on it. He's so confident of proving you wrong. Anyway, you're in deep doo and I'd suggest you think about packing up your sheep. And you're not to speak to the press. They're all over the place.'

Jimmy watched as Hamish walked sadly away. He felt in sudden need of a drink. He went to the local pub near headquarters and ordered a double whisky. He turned and surveyed the bar; his eyes lighted on Tam Tamworth, nicknamed 'the pig', because with his large ears and beefy face, short nose and pursed lips, he did look piggy.

Jimmy strolled over to him. 'I'm not supposed to speak to the press,' he said in a low voice, 'but see if you can use this. Mention my name and I'll have to kill you.'

'So is it about thon murder?' asked Tam.

'Aye, thanks to our Hamish Macbeth, it may turn out to be two murders. Say you happened to have been passing the garage at the side o' headquarters last night, this is what you heard.' He rapidly described Hamish's suspicions, saying that if Macbeth turned out to be right, he should be getting a commendation rather than suspension.

'Man, what a story,' said Tam. 'I'm off. I can get it into the morning paper.'

Thanks to an excellent sports section, the *Strathbane Journal* had a good circulation. Daviot read it next morning with a sinking heart. Blair went out and got drunk, praying between drinks that the DNA would prove Hamish wrong. Headquarters was besieged by press and television demanding a statement. Hamish Macbeth was nowhere to be found. He had packed up his camping equipment, taken his pets, and set off to hide out in the moors.

The previous forensic team had all been sacked because of too many reports of drunkenness. A new laboratory had been built and an expert from Glasgow coaxed up to head the new team. They worked long hours and at last had a full report. The blood in the sidecar belonged to Pete Ray. The fingerprints on the wallet and candlesticks had obviously been put there after the man was dead because it looked as if fingers had simply been pressed down on the items. Pete would have grasped the candlesticks, not put a neat set of fingerprints on them. His neck had not been broken by a fall; someone had broken it by twisting his head back. There were signs that Pete's body had then been stuffed into the sidecar.

And there was worse. Angus Forrest had said there was no use bothering forensics with the motorcycle and sidecar. It was an open-and-shut case, in his opinion, and his superiors had told him to wrap it up fast.

Jimmy was told to get hold of Hamish Macbeth, return him to his duties, and keep away from the press. Phoning Hamish on his mobile, Jimmy gave him the good news. 'But you're to keep away for another week,' he said, 'until Daviot thinks the press have stopped looking for you.'

'Suits me,' said Hamish laconically, turning sausages on a frying pan balanced on a camp stove outside his tent.

'Aye, but there's something else. You'd better clear out that spare room at the station. You're to get a constable. His name is Torlich McBain and he's a wee sneak. I think he's supposed to keep an eye on you and report to Blair. He's a bit o' a Bible-basher. He'll preach you the word.'

* * *

17

Milly Davenport had enjoyed a few days of what she guiltily thought of as freedom. The women from the village were kind. She loved the gossip over cups of tea, and she loved the company.

They worked like a pack of guard dogs to keep the press away from her and give Blair a hard time. Blair had worked out a scenario in his fat brain where Milly had a jealous lover and would have browbeaten her had not the women sent a letter of complaint to Daviot.

But on the morning that Hamish Macbeth returned to his police station, Captain Henry Davenport's sister, Miss Philomena Davenport, arrived at Milly's house. 'I'm come to stay with you, Milly,' she said. 'It's what my dear brother would have wanted.'

Philomena was a tall woman with big hands and feet. She had cropped grey hair and slightly prominent pale-green eyes. She was dressed in gear she considered suitable for the Highlands: knee breeches, lovat wool socks, a green Army sweater, and a leather fleece.

She disapproved of Milly 'consorting with the local peasantry' and so banned them from the house.

Milly felt she had lost one bully only to find another.

Hamish watched sadly as a scrap dealer from Alness drove off with the contents of his spare room: an old fridge, bits of a plough, rusting screwdrivers, two old televisions, and myriad iron bits and pieces. Although he had previously cleaned it out, when the female constable who had nearly tricked him into marriage was supposed to take the room and was billeted at the manse instead, he had just put everything back in again. Mrs Wellington, the minister's wife, arrived with a cleaning squad. A bed, wardrobe, and side table were delivered from a Strathbane shop, the bill to be footed by the police.

Torlich, nicknamed Tolly, arrived to take up residence. He had never risen in the ranks due to failing all the necessary exams. He was small for a policeman, with a wrinkled, sagging grey face and weak watery eyes.

'I'll let you get settled in,' said Hamish. 'I'm off to Drim to have a word with Mrs Davenport.'

'That should be left to your superiors,' said Tolly.

He had been told Hamish Macbeth was an easy-going layabout. But the hazel eyes that looked down into his own were as hard as stone. 'You will do what you are told, Constable,' said Hamish. 'In future, you address me as "sir". You have the day to get your things unpacked.'

He turned on his heel and marched out, followed by Sonsie and Lugs. Tolly decided to spend the time going through Hamish's papers and belongings. If he was a spy, then he would be a good spy. God had given him this chance to prove his mettle.

Hamish drove to the captain's house in Drim and rang the doorbell. A tall tweedy woman answered it. 'I am Miss Davenport, my poor brother's sister,' she announced, 'and Mrs Davenport has had enough of the police. Good day to you.'

The door began to close. Hamish put his boot in it.

'Neffer let it be said that a lady like yourself is impeding the police in a murder inquiry,' remarked Hamish, the sudden sibilance of his Highland accent showing he was annoyed.

'Who is it?' Milly appeared behind her sister-in-law. 'Oh, I remember you. Please come in.'

'Milly, I do not think you are up to any more questioning,' said Philomena.

'As long as it isn't that man called Blair, I don't mind. Come in. Please leave us, Philomena.'

She led the way into the kitchen. 'My name is Hamish Macbeth, from Lochdubh,' said Hamish.

'Yes, I remember. I phoned you.'

'You're probably tired of questions . . .'

'I don't mind,' said Milly, 'so long as you don't shout at me.'

'I am not the shouting kind.'

'Tea?'

'That would be grand.'

Milly plugged in the kettle. Hamish moved quickly to the kitchen door and jerked it open. Philomena, who had been leaning against it on the other side, nearly fell into the kitchen. 'A bit o' privacy, please,' said Hamish and shut the door in her face.

'I wish I could do that,' said Milly mournfully. 'She is so like her brother.'

'Well, it'll take you a good bit of time to get over your husband's death.'

'Milk?'

'No, chust plain. Thank you. Now, Mrs Davenport, there is one odd thing. Why would your husband leave his wallet behind, or do you think it was taken from his body?'

'I don't know. I don't think he planned to be away for long, but it was odd that he said if anyone called looking for him, I should say he had gone abroad.'

'That does sound as if he was frightened of someone.'

'Well, he did take against people. He had a phone call the evening before. When we lived in Surrey, he did annoy people.'

'In what way?'

'Well, he often had get-rich-quick ideas and would try to rope in some of his old Army friends. I remember one of them wanted money back and shouted a lot.'

'Who was it?'

'I can't rightly remember.'

'So he could have tricked someone else out of money?'

'It's possible. Oh, dear. Maybe they'll come looking for me.'

'I shouldnae think so. Would you like me to put a guard on the house?'

'It would certainly make me feel better.'

'I'll send someone over. It doesn't matter what the weather's like. Keep him outside the house. We'll put him on night duty. Why did you come up here?'

'Henry started going through house advertisements for property in the north of Scotland. I didn't want to go. I liked Guildford. We had a nice little bungalow and I had a few friends.'

'I want you to think hard and make me out a list of his old Army friends. Which regiment?'

'The Surrey Infantry.'

'I won't be bothering you any more just now. I'll call tomorrow. You look as if you could do with some fresh air. Why don't you walk down to the village with me?'

'Philomena doesn't like me associating with the locals.'

'Then she'll chust need to lump it. Get your coat.'

Chapter Two

The Bustle in a House
The Morning after Death
Is solemnest of industries
Enacted upon Earth –

The Sweeping up the Heart
And putting Love away
We shall not want to use again
Until Eternity

— EMILY DICKINSON

'You'd get a rare view of the loch if it weren't for these bushes and trees,' commented Hamish as they walked down the short drive.

'I wouldn't know how to begin to get rid of them,' said Milly.

'I know a couple o' forestry workers who would be glad of a bit of extra work. They can keep the wood as payment.'

'I don't know what Philomena would think . . .'

'It's your house now. Not hers,' said Hamish sharply. 'I assume you inherit it?'

'Yes, the police left me the will. Philomena phoned the solicitor in Inverness. She was quite angry about that. We had a joint account so money won't be a problem, says the bank.'

'And did he leave a lot of money?'

'Enough to keep me for a few years, but after that I'll need to try to sell this place. I will get his Army pension, of course.'

'Has your sister-in-law any money of her own?'

'Yes, she is quite rich, I believe. You see, poor Henry's parents had a falling-out with him and left everything to Philomena.'

'It seems to me, Mrs Davenport, that she should leave quite soon.'

'I daren't ask her.'

'You can't have her staying on, unless of course she's helping with the household expenses.'

'Well, she isn't,' said Milly in a faltering voice. 'The trouble is, Mr Macbeth, I am just like Henry always said I was – no backbone. What a depressing loch that is! Like a long black finger pointing out to the Atlantic.'

Although a pale sun was shining down on the huddle of village houses that lay on a little plateau above the sea, the light did not penetrate the dark waters of the loch where the steep mountains on either side plunged straight down, their scree-covered flanks only holding a few stunted bushes.

In the general store, Hamish stood patiently whilst Milly talked shyly to Ailsa Kennedy, the red-haired wife of the owner, and to two of the villagers, Edie Aubrey and Alice MacQueen.

Ailsa asked, 'What do you do about the cleaning? That's a rare big house to dust.'

Milly blushed. 'We only used a few of the rooms. I do what I can.'

'You puir wee lassie,' said Ailsa. 'You need help. We'll be along this afternoon.'

'I d-don't know what my sister-in-law . . .'

'Nonsense. She'll be glad o' the help. Will you be having a wake after the funeral?'

'I don't know when the procurator fiscal is going to release the body. Besides, Henry did not believe in anything.'

'We'll get the Church of Scotland minister,' said Edie. 'He would rather send a body to the next world with a Christian burial than have the poor soul put in the ground with nothing at all. I'll ask him.'

Milly began to cry, tears running down her face. A chair was found for her. Ailsa rushed off to the kitchen at the back and returned with a mug of tea into which she had put a generous slug of whisky. 'Put that down ye,' she ordered.

When Milly had recovered, she said, 'You are all so kind, but as to the cleaning, I am sure Philomena will not allow it.'

'We'll see about that,' said Ailsa. 'Everything fixed up wi' the lawyer?'

'Oh, yes.'

'That would be Byles and Cox in Strathbane?'

'Oh, no, Tarry and Wilkins in Inverness.'

More women came into the shop, crowding around Milly and offering support. Ailsa nipped quietly into the back shop and phoned Philomena. 'This is Tarry and Wilkins, solicitors,' she said in a prim voice. 'Mr Tarry has a letter left for you by Mr Henry Davenport with instructions it was to be handed to you personally on his death.'

'Is it another will?' asked Philomena hopefully.

'That we don't know, Miss Davenport. Only you can open the letter.'

'I'm setting off right away,' said Philomena.

Hamish returned with Milly to her home, folowed by six women carrying dusters, mops, and brushes. Milly was terrified. She felt sure that Philomena would order them all away.

But her car was not there, and there was a note left for her on the kitchen table.

'Dear Milly,' she read. 'Called away on urgent business. Back this evening.'

Hamish was amused. He was sure Ailsa had something to do with it.

'Mrs Davenport,' he said, 'I will call on you tomorrow. Do try to find me a list of your husband's friends.'

'I promise,' said Milly, and Hamish left behind him a cheery clatter of gossiping women.

When Hamish got back to the police station, he walked into his office and immediately sensed that everything had been searched.

Tolly came in and stood waiting. 'Who are you spying for?' demanded Hamish. 'Blair?'

'I would not stoop to do anything so low,' protested Tolly. 'I am a Christian and I always do my duty.'

'Then you can start now. Get yourself over to Drim and stand guard on that house all night. I'll relieve you in the morning.'

'I haven't had any sleep, sir!'

'Get to it or I'll put in a report on you. Do you think I don't know when my papers have been searched? Go to it!'

Philomena arrived back from Inverness in a rage after having been firmly told that there was no letter for her, nor had they phoned. Milly was seated in the drawing room, watching television. She cringed when Philomena shouted, 'What's been going on here?'

The once dingy room smelled fresh and clean. Several pieces of the Swedish-type furniture had been removed and replaced with shabby but comfortable chairs the ladies of Drim had found in the attics. Milly switched off the television and said, 'The local ladies came to help me clear the house. I never liked that modern furniture, and it never suited this room.'

'It was my poor brother's choice. Get it back.'

The doorbell rang. 'I'll get it,' said Philomena grimly. She opened the door and glared down at Tolly, who gave her an ingratiating smile. 'I'm here to guard the house,' he said. 'I wondered if I could be having a chair to sit on and maybe a cup of tea.'

'No,' said Philomena, and slammed the door in his face.

When she returned to the drawing room, Milly was just replacing the phone receiver. 'Who was at the door?' she asked.

'Just some policeman. He says he's here to guard the house. Who were you phoning?'

'Really, you go too far,' said Milly. The doorbell rang again. Milly darted past her sister-in-law. 'That will be for me.'

It was Ailsa. 'Everything all right?'

'Sort of,' said Milly.

'Don't let her bully you. See you tomorrow.'

'Who was that?' demanded Philomena.

'Just a friend,' said Milly.

'Now, listen to me,' said Philomena, looming over her. 'My brother believed in people knowing their place. He would turn in his grave if he thought you were consorting with the villagers.'

Milly sighed. 'He's not in his grave yet.' And with a sudden spurt of courage, 'If you go on nagging like that, Philomena, someone will murder *you*!'

Philomena slowly backed away. 'I'm going to my room,' she said. She felt suddenly nervous. What did she really know of Milly?

Tolly had retreated to his police car and started the engine and heater running. When he felt warm again, he switched the engine off. He had hidden the police car a little way down the hill where he could still get a good view of the house. His eyes began to droop. The night was very still. Then he thought he saw a black shadow approaching the house. He straightened up and slowly got out of the police car without slamming the door behind him.

Taking his baton, he crept towards the house, his heart beating hard. He knew all of a sudden that he had been neglecting his duty by sitting in his car some yards away from the entrance.

He scurried up the short drive, looking to left and right. Tolly decided to call for backup. He wanted to stay alive to collect his pension in four years' time. He took out his mobile phone. Then from behind him, the police radio in the car – which he had forgotten to switch off – crackled into life reporting a burglary down at the docks in Strathbane. 'I need backup,' he yelled into his phone. 'Intruder at Drim!'

Something heavy struck him on the back of the head and he fell unconscious.

Lights went on in the house. Milly had heard Tolly's call; it had awakened her from an uneasy sleep. Philomena joined her on the landing. 'Call the police,' she whispered.

'Haven't you got a mobile?' asked Milly.

'It's downstairs in my handbag.'

'Mine, too, and the phone's in the hall. What are we going to do?'

Hanging on to each other, they crept down the stairs. Milly grabbed the phone in the hall and called the police.

Hamish Macbeth was awakened by the shrill sound of the telephone. He struggled out of bed, ran to the office, and listened in alarm when he was told there was something bad happening at the Davenport house in Drim.

When he got there, the small figure of Tolly was being carried into an ambulance. Police

Inspector Mary Benson was in charge of operations. She was a matronly looking woman whose grey hair and rosy cheeks belied a ruthless efficiency.

'What on earth happened to the wee man?' asked Hamish.

'Someone bashed him on the head,' said Mary. 'He was just shouting something into his phone about an intruder when it happened.'

'Is he bad?'

'Looks bad. We can only hope for the best. You should have done the job yourself, Macbeth. His police radio was blaring away, enough to alert anybody that the house was watched.'

'Whose fault is it that I was sent a dangerously inept policeman, ma'am?'

'Don't get cheeky with me. Join the search.'

'Yes, ma'am,' said Hamish gloomily.

'We'd best get these women off to a safe house for a bit.'

Hamish went up the drive and round to the kitchen door, shining his torch on the ground, searching for footprints. But the ground was hard and dry, and a lot of the path was covered by weeds and heather. The captain, thought Hamish, must have had something that the murderer desperately wanted. And how had the man arrived? Had he left a car somewhere and walked over the hills?

31

He would need to return as soon as it was daylight and search again.

Milly had always wondered how any human being could take the life of another. But after a week in the safe house in Strathbane with Philomena, she felt she understood. The safe house was actually a small flat. She had to share a bedroom with her sister-in-law. At first, Philomena would not let her go out at all, saying it was not safe. Milly waited until she had fallen asleep one afternoon and the police-woman on guard outside in her car had fallen asleep as well, and walked down into the centre of the town.

The body of her husband was to be released the following week, and she would be returning home then to prepare for the funeral. She had given Hamish Macbeth the names and addresses of any of her husband's old Army friends that she could find after writing off to them herself and inviting them to the funeral. So far, not one had replied, even with a letter of condolence. Philomena had said that her brother had been very popular and that the police were probably intercepting the mail for security reasons, which police headquarters denied. 'Well, they would say that,' said Philomena, who felt she was always right about everything.

Milly was just wondering whether to buy herself the first pair of high heels she had had in ages – the captain had not approved of her wearing high heels – when a voice behind her asked, 'Mrs Davenport?'

She swung round and backed nervously against a shop window. The man facing her looked like a large pig. 'Yes, I'm one o' thae dreadful reporters,' he said cheerily. 'My name's Tam Tamworth. Fancy a drink?'

'I mustn't speak to the press,' said Milly primly.

'Och, it's just the wee dram and I'll gie ye a piece o' paper saying I won't print anything you say.'

Milly wavered. Then she thought of going back to that nasty little flat and being cooped up with Philomena. 'All right,' she said.

'We'll go to the Grand Hotel bar,' said Tam. 'Nice and posh. It's just a few steps away.'

The cocktail bar of the Grand Hotel was a veritable symphony to Scottish bad taste. The walls were draped in tartan cloth and hung with plastic claymores and targes. There was a huge, badly executed portrait of Bonnie Prince Charlie behind the bar. The plastic tables were made to look like tree trunks and covered in tartan coasters.

'What'll it be?' asked Tam.

'Just an orange juice.'

'An orange juice after what you've been through? Have a Tartan Blaster.'

'What's that?'

'Jist a mild cocktail.'

'All right,' said Milly boldly.

The Tartan Blaster arrived. It was a bright-red drink decorated with two tartan umbrellas.

Tam had a double whisky. 'What do you think of Strathbane?' he asked.

'It's a bit, well, run-down,' said Milly shyly.

'Didn't use tae be. Before the European Union got its claws into the fishing industry, this used to be a lively place. Now everyone's on the dole. I'll be covering your man's funeral if that's all right wi' you.'

'I don't suppose I can stop you,' said Milly. The liquor in the cocktail was sending a warm glow right down to her stomach. 'And I can't discuss anything with you, about the murder I mean.'

'I'll tell you one thing. It's just come through. Trust Hamish Macbeth to get it right. Poor wee Pete Ray was murdered and by the same chap who did in your husband.'

Milly shuddered and took a large gulp of her drink. 'That's awful. Am I in danger?'

'I would say that whoever tried to get into the house the other day will be too frightened to come back.'

'I'm in a safe house,' said Milly. 'Well, it's rather a safe flat – me and my sister-in-law. I don't think I can take much more of it. We're under each other's feet all day long.'

'Then just go back to Drim. They can't stop you.'

The police were searching for Milly, alerted by a frantic Philomena screaming down the phone. Like practically every town in Britain, Strathbane was well served by CCTV cameras. A quick scan soon picked up the slight form of Milly being joined by Tam Tamworth and followed them to the Grand Hotel.

Just as Milly was finishing her drink, two policemen and a policewoman came hurrying into the bar. Said the leading policeman, 'You must return to the safe house, Mrs Davenport, and you should not be talking to the press. Come with us. Your sister-in-law is worried frantic about you.'

Milly cracked. She shouted, 'I am not going back to that grubby flat. I am going home and you can't stop me!'

'Attagirl,' said Tam. 'You tell 'em.'

'I must remind you, Mrs Davenport . . .'

Milly got to her feet. 'And I must say that if I am cooped up in that small flat with Philomena for one more day, I will murder her!'

The bar had filled up since Milly had first entered it. Everyone was listening avidly. 'Mr Tamworth,' said Milly, 'would you please take me back to the flat and then escort me to Drim?'

'Glad to.'

'You can't do that!' protested the policeman.

'Oh, yes I can,' said the normally mild Milly, full of Tartan Blaster.

'You've never seen such a change in anyone,' chortled Jimmy Anderson when he met up with Hamish outside the house in Drim. 'Tam's got his foot in the door there and he's not leaving. Philomena is ranting and raving. Have you found anything?'

'Not a thing. I've been searching around since early light. Well, there is one thing. Five miles away, up on the Lairg road, there's a Forestry Commission road going up through the trees. There's a muddy bit at the entrance with tyre tracks. They've taken a cast off to the lab. Someone could have parked there and then walked over the moors. Have you managed to get rid of Tam?'

'Finally. But he'll be back. Mrs Davenport seems to have taken a shine to the pig, mostly because Tam is so deliciously rude to Philomena.'

'Have you checked up on the old family friends?'

'Surrey police are on to it. Stonewalling all around. Either that or don't speak ill of the dead. You'd think headquarters would all be pleased that you turned out to be right and there are two murders but the way Blair is going on, you'd think you'd done them your-self. Have you considered the locals, Hamish?'

'Not for a moment. Why?'

'They're all a bit weird up here.'

'As far as I know, the captain never had any-thing to do with any of them apart from Hugh Mackenzie who supplies the peat.'

'And what does he say?'

'Says he had no quarrel with the captain. Says the captain paid him by letting him take as much peat as he wanted for himself.'

Inside the house, Tam, who had shut Philomena outside the kitchen, was saying earnestly to Milly, 'I promise you this. I won't write a word until after the murderer is caught. I have great faith in Macbeth. Background stuff, exclusively to me. And that'll keep the rest of the press away from you.'

'All right,' said Milly. 'And will you do something for me?'

'What?'

Milly looked at him shyly. 'Will you take me to see a film next week?'

'Sure. Which one?'

'Anything will do. I want a bit of escape. I feel I've been cooped up in here like a prisoner ever since Henry moved us here.'

Tam's large ears turned a bit pink with gratification. He noticed for the first time that

Milly had a sort of old-fashioned prettiness about her.

'Now,' he said, 'the police have taken away all the papers. Is there anything in this big place they might have missed?'

'I shouldn't think so. The search was very thorough.'

Philomena moved quietly away from the kitchen door. Suppose there was some evidence in the house and she found it. The village women had been up in the attics, getting pieces of furniture. Maybe there was something now uncovered that they and the police had missed.

She went quietly up the stairs. A wind had risen outside, moaning and screaming around the house. The village women had been thorough. The attics were clean and dusted. Philomena began to search, avoiding places like old trunks and suitcases that the police had surely rummaged through.

There were three attics. One had obviously been a nursery in the old days. A soldier's campaign chest stood against the wall by a small barred window. She stared at it thoughtfully. She suddenly remembered their father having bought it at an auction, saying it had belonged to an officer in the Crimean War. And, she remembered with excitement, it had a secret drawer.

38

She found it by opening a top drawer and taking it out. Behind it was another little drawer. She opened it and found a bundle of letters – and the letters looked fairly new.

She sat down on an old nursing chair and began to read. The letters were from lawyers, angrily demanding money back that Henry owed their clients. But there was one from the man himself. 'Pay up, Henry, or I'll kill you, you damn cheat,' it said.

Philomena had felt humiliated by the arrival of Tam in Milly's life. She had not liked the way Hamish Macbeth had treated her, either. She was consumed by a desire to show them all up; to show that she, Philomena, could find a murderer. Her mind worked fast. She would contact this man and arrange to meet him in a public place, and she would take a powerful tape recorder with her and see if she could get enough evidence before she went to the police. She put the lawyers' letters back in the drawer, dusted off any prints she might have left in the room, and went quietly down the stairs.

There was no police guard outside. Head-quarters had decreed that if Mrs Davenport was foolish enough to leave the safe house, then she would just have to take the consequences.

Philomena walked outside and into the shelter of the shrubbery. Far above her, the monkey puzzle tree groaned and creaked and swayed in the gale while ragged clouds raced across a small moon. With a little smile on her face, Philomena took out her mobile phone.

Tam left and Philomena said curtly after supper that she was going to have an early night and planned to go to Inverness shopping on the following day.

No sooner had she gone to bed than the doorbell rang. 'Who is it?' called Milly through the letter box.

'It's me, Hamish Macbeth. Mind if I come in for a moment?'

Milly opened the door. 'Has anything happened?'

'No, no,' said Hamish soothingly. 'I was just wondering, is there anywhere the captain might have hidden anything, like papers?'

'I think the house has been searched from top to bottom.' They walked into the kitchen together.

'I spend most of the time in here now,' said Milly. 'It's warmer, and here I'm not haunted by the vision of poor Henry up the chimney.'

The kitchen was old-fashioned with a stone floor: Belfast sinks and a large dresser holding willow-pattern plates against one wall and a Raeburn cooker against another.

'You haven't really had time,' said Hamish, 'to have a proper think. Anything anywhere? The attics?'

'I left the search to the police.'

40

'Mind if I go upstairs and have a look?'

'Go ahead. At least there's electric light in the attics. You'll be able to see all right.'

Hamish checked around the attics looking for hiding places such as loose floorboards. He was about to give up as he was standing in the nursery when his eyes fell on the campaign chest. Although the village women had cleaned well, the attics were not at all insulated, and scurrying draughts had begun to cover objects already with a thin coating of dust. The campaign chest against the wall was the one object free of dust.

He went back down to the kitchen. 'Mrs Davenport,' he said, 'there's a chest up in the old nursery against the wall. Know anything about it?'

'I don't think so. I'll come back up with you and have a look.'

In the nursery, Milly surveyed the chest. 'Oh, that. Henry was proud of that. It belonged to his father.'

'I 'member an auctioneer in Inverness telling me these old chests often had a secret drawer.'

'Henry didn't mention anything.'

'Well, someone's been having a look. Let me see if I can remember. It's maybe at the back of one of the drawers. He said you aye look for a shorter drawer. Here we are! Right at the top.' He took a pair of latex gloves out of his pocket and put them on. His nimble fingers found the secret drawer. Hamish scanned the lawyers' letters and let out a low whistle.

'What is it?' asked Milly.

'These are letters from four lawyers all demanding money for their clients, money they say that Henry borrowed and was refusing to pay back. I'll need tae rush these ower tae Strathbane,' said Hamish, his accent getting broader in his excitement. 'This place is cleaner than the other attics. Has anyone else been up here? Your sister-in-law? Tam?'

'Tam certainly hasn't. Philomena might have been up here.'

'I'm afraid I'll have to ask you to get her and ask her.'

'But she's gone to bed! And she'll be so angry at being woken up.'

'Just show me her bedroom door and I'll do the rest.'

Philomena was furiously haughty in her denials. Was she not going to be allowed to sleep?

Hamish carefully examined the front door and kitchen door but could see no signs of any type of break-in. But perhaps the captain had his house keys on his dead body and the killer had taken them away.

'I'll get a locksmith along in the morning to change the locks,' he said, 'and get a deadbolt put on the kitchen door. I'll give you a receipt for these letters and then get over to Strathbane and hand them in as evidence.'

In his Land Rover, he switched on the overhead light and, taking out his notebook, made a careful note of the lawyers' names and addresses and the names of their clients. They were all down in Surrey. He wished he could go there himself. It would mean he would not have to wait until a report came back from the Surrey police. But one of them might have come north and stayed locally before contacting the captain.

He studied the clients' names: Ferdinand Castle, Thomas Bromley, John Sanders, and Charles Prosser. Then he set off for Strathbane.

He preferred to deal with Jimmy, but Jimmy had gone home. He telephoned him. Jimmy groaned and said he'd be back at the office in a few moments.

When he arrived, he exclaimed over the letters, 'Now we might get somewhere. A secret drawer! It's like something out o' Enid Blyton.'

'It's like something out o' the *Antiques Roadshow*,' said Hamish. 'I mind being amazed at the number of old pieces o' furniture wi' secret drawers. But forensics had better go back and have a go at that attic. Someone's been in there, and I would think that someone was there after the village women did a' the cleaning.'

Jimmy leaned back in his chair, yawned, and put his battered brogues up on the desk.

'Don't you think sweet little Milly or that great bullying sister-in-law might have found something they're not telling us about?'

'I hope not,' said Hamish. 'Surely neither woman would want to go after a ruthless killer on her own.'

Philomena arrived in the bar of the Dancing Scotsman Hotel on the banks of the River Ness at one o'clock the following day. Her heart was beating hard. For one little moment, a grain of common sense was telling her that she was putting herself at risk. But she banished it. She would show them that she was sharper and brighter than anyone in the police force, particularly Hamish Macbeth. And the bar was crowded. She had nothing to fear.

By quarter past one, she was beginning to feel like a fool. Of course the murderer would not come. But he might be waiting outside to follow her and accost her on a quiet stretch of the road home.

With a sinking heart, Philomena realized that, for her own safety, she would need to go straight to Inverness police. What could she say that would not make her look like the dangerous idiot she now felt?

A woman sat down opposite her. 'Do you mind?' she asked. 'All the other seats seem to be full.'

'I'm waiting for someone,' said Philomena harshly. But the woman was middle-aged and respectable, plump and motherly and wearing a large hat. 'Oh, well, just until my companion turns up.' Philomena decided to give it another fifteen minutes. She could not bear to fail.

'Aren't the shops busy,' said the woman. 'I remember when Inverness was just a quiet country town.'

The woman ordered a vodka and Red Bull when the waiter came up. 'You haven't touched yours, dear,' she said to Philomena.

'Oh, I don't feel like drinking.'

Philomena's bag was open on the seat beside her. 'Look at that man!' said her companion suddenly. 'What is he doing?'

Looking out the window, all Philomena could see were innocent-looking passers-by. She did not see the woman reach over and deftly extract the letter from her handbag. Nor did she see her slipping something into her drink.

'Cheers!' said the woman when her drink arrived.

Philomena took a sip. 'I couldn't see anything odd,' she said.

'I could swear there was a man exposing himself. Disgusting, I call it. No morals these days.'

Philomena made up her mind. He was not going to come. She took a strong gulp of her

45

gin and tonic to give herself courage to move. But she began to feel dizzy and faint.

'Are you all right?' she heard her companion ask. 'Someone help me get her outside into the fresh air.'

'No,' said Philomena weakly. 'No.'

The bar tilted and swung before her eyes. Outside she faintly heard her companion say, 'Help me get her into her husband's car. That's right. She'll be right as rain once he gets her home.'

Philomena's last conscious memory was of a deep voice saying, 'Mistake, Philomena. Bad, bad mistake.'

Chapter Three

Swans sing before they die: t'were no bad thing
Should certain persons die before they sing
— SAMUEL TAYLOR COLERIDGE

Philomena slowly recovered consciousness. She tried to move, but her wrists were chained and padlocked to a bed. Her throat was dry. 'Help,' she croaked.

'I will let you go,' said a man's voice from the corner of the room, 'if you swear to me you did not show that letter to the police.'

'I swear ... I promise you on my life.'

'If you've lied to me, then your life is what you'll be losing. Do you understand?'

'Yes, yes.'

'Shut your eyes.'

Philomena heard two clicks as the handcuffs were released. 'You will find your car a bit away from this bothie on the Struie Pass. You will stay here for ten minutes and then go. If you so much as utter a word about this to anyone, I know where to find you.'

'Yes, please,' begged Philomena.

She heard the door of the bothie close. After a few minutes, she tried to sit up. She felt dizzy and weak. She could barely remember anything except sitting in that bar in Inverness and the woman opposite urging her to look out the window.

She finally swung her legs down on to the floor. The place was filthy and looked as if it had not been used, except maybe by school-boys or vagrants, for years. There was a strong smell of excrement and urine. The mattress she had been lying on was soiled, with broken springs curling through the torn covering in places.

A rickety table held a bottle of mineral water and the remains of a bottle of whisky. She felt so parched, she opened the bottle and drank the water.

She did not care whether ten minutes had passed or not. Philomena staggered out into the spring sunlight. Over the heather, she recognized her car parked up on the road.

She hurried towards it, sometimes tripping and falling, but always rising and forging on to safety.

A watcher lowered his powerful binoculars. 'Think she'll keep her mouth shut?' asked the woman beside him.

'No.'

'Think she drank the water?'

'Probably. That drug you slipped into her drink causes a tremendous thirst. Let her set off and then we'll follow her to make sure. We can always take her out before she reaches Drim. Did you put all the flammable stuff in the back?'

'Yes.'

'She's off. Let's go.'

The Struie Pass, the old road into Sutherland, is full of hairpin bends, but at the top it commands the most beautiful view as Sutherland lies in front and below: ranges of blue mountains and lochs stretching into the distance.

Philomena kept blinking. Lights were flashing before her eyes. At the viewpoint, she suddenly saw a smooth dual carriageway stretching out in front of her. People seemed to be dancing on it, which was odd, but all she thought of was escape. She pressed her foot down hard on the accelerator and plunged right off the edge of the Struie Pass. The car rolled and tumbled and finally hit a rock where it burst into flames, a fireball from hell.

'She drank the water,' said the man with satisfaction.

'Aren't you being a bit over-elaborate? All that LSD?' asked his companion. 'She probably told someone.'

'No, she didn't. I know Philomena. She had a tape recorder in her bag. She was going to play detective. If she'd told her sister-in-law or the police, they'd have been after me by now. Now, let's go. I've got to cover my tracks. We'll throw her phone along with that tape recorder in the nearest peat bog.'

'Look, she may have said something to her sister-in-law.'

'Not her, pompous cow.'

Milly enjoyed a relatively peaceful day. But as evening approached and there was no sign of her sister-in-law, she began to fret. She went up to Philomena's room. All her clothes were still hanging in the wardrobe.

She phoned Hamish Macbeth. 'It's not like her. For days, she hasn't left me alone for a minute, and now she hasn't even phoned. She said she was going to Inverness to do some shopping.'

'Have you a photograph of her?'

'I might have an old one somewhere.'

'Look for it. What was she wearing?'

'A heather-mixture tweed suit with brogues.'

'Hat?'

'No hat.'

'What was she driving?'

'A Ford Escort.' Milly gave Hamish the registration number.

'Phone me as soon as she gets back,' he said, 'but I'll let you know if we find her.'

Milly said goodbye, put down the receiver, and sat staring at it. Then she phoned Tam Tamworth. He was not in the office, but he had left her his mobile phone number.

'Now then,' said Tam when she told him about her missing sister-in-law, 'I wouldnae put it past thon wumman to stay away jist to frighten you. But I'll go look.'

The next morning, a family stopped at the viewpoint on the Struie Pass to admire the view: father, mother, and two small children, the Renfrew family up from Glasgow.

'Aren't the Highlands just grand,' said Ian Renfrew, taking his binoculars and getting out of the car. 'Come and see the view.'

'You go,' said his wife, huddled in the front seat. 'It's as cold as hell out there.'

A wind was screaming across the heather. The children in the backseat, Zak, age ten, and Gypsy, age nine, were listening on their iPods and ignored their father.

He swept the horizon with his binoculars, first towards Western Fearn Point on the Kyle of Sutherland and across the kyle to Creich Mains and then focused them on the burnt-out wreck of a car far down one of the braes below, just before he was preparing to put the binoculars away.

His eyes sharpened as he adjusted the focus. He could see a black mass inside the wreckage that looked like a body; a little way away on the heather was one shoe.

He felt a bit sick. He got into the car and took out his phone. He called the police and reported that there was a burnt-out wreck of a car below the viewpoint on the Struie Pass and he was sure there was a body in it. His wife stared at him in alarm.

'We've tae stay right here,' he said.

The children finally unplugged their iPods and whined, 'Why are we stopped?'

'Your father's seen a dead body in a car down the brae and we're to wait for the police,' said Mrs Renfrew.

'Cool!' chorused the delighted children.

Hamish arrived on the scene. A forensic team was having difficulty erecting a tent over the car and body because of the strength of the wind. 'What do you think, Hamish?' asked Jimmy. 'Lost concentration and went off the road?'

'Not a hope wi' a fire like that,' said Hamish. 'It's only in the movies that they burst into flames. Some accelerant was in that car. It's her, all right. They cleaned the number plate and it matches with hers. Damn! I'll tell you what probably happened. She found one letter in that secret drawer and decided to play detective herself. Now she said she was going to Inverness. If she thought she was so clever, she'd arrange to meet whoever in a public place. Where?'

'Shopping mall?'

'Probably some hotel bar,' said Hamish. 'And let's hope it's some hotel bar with CCTV.'

A shocked and weeping Milly had found a photograph of Philomena addressing a Women's Institute meeting. It was a good clear shot, and it was circulated to the police and the newspapers.

A waitress from the Dancing Scotsman came forward to say she recognized Philomena. She had been talking to a woman. Then she seemed to take faint and the woman had helped her outside. Another witness turned up. He had seen a woman answering Philomena's description being helped into a four-wheel drive with tinted windows. No, he could not see who was driving.

The police were excited. They felt it was only a matter of time before they caught the killer. There was no CCTV inside the hotel bar, but they had a full description of the woman with Philomena.

'Fix yourself a drink, darling,' called the woman who had helped to kidnap Philomena.

'I must get this stuff off.' She went into the bathroom. She removed pads from her cheeks and layers of foam rubber that had given her a plump figure. She would have removed them immediately after Philomena had gone to her death but he had said to wait until they were back in Edinburgh. It had made her uneasy, because they must have some sort of description of her by now. She was revealed as a slim woman in her forties.

Her flat was in the Royal Mile, in a tall tenement in the Canongate. She reappeared from the bathroom, wrapped in a dressing gown. 'It's hot in here,' she said. 'You didn't need to light a fire.'

She flung up the sash window and took a great gulp of fresh air. He seized her by the ankles and thrust her through the window. With a long wailing scream, she fell to her death below. He raked red-hot coals out from the fire and piled newspapers on top then fled the flat, easing into the crowds going up and down the Royal Mile, forcing himself to walk at a leisurely pace. At the North Bridge, he hailed a taxi to where he had parked the four-wheel drive. He had already removed the false number plates. He drove out to a small, old cottage he had rented, miles out into the countryside, and there he started to work to restore his appearance to normal, tearing off a false moustache and beard. He would let things all go quiet for a few months and then see about getting back that money Captain Henry Davenport had conned him out of.

At first, with so many clues, it seemed only a matter of time before the killer was found. But the police came up against dead end after dead end. No one connected the death of a high-class prostitute and a fire in an apartment in the Royal Mile with the Sutherland murders.

Surrey police had interviewed the four lawyers' clients: Ferdinand Castle, Thomas Bromley, John Sanders, and Charles Prosser. The captain had fired them up with a get-rich-quick idea. He said that mining for gold was about to start over at Ben Nevis. He produced geological surveys. He said he needed more money to invest to get them all in on the ground floor, but to secure the deal it would need to be in cash. The four had loaned him close to £750,000. After some time, they began to become suspicious and demanded the money back. The captain had blustered and said they would be paid in full. The lawyers' letters had been sent to his home in Guildford. Shortly after that, he had sold his house, quietly – no estate agent's board outside – and disappeared.

The four men all had cast-iron alibis. Not one of them had been out of Guildford for months. They swore they thought that Captain

Davenport was a sound man and had been a brave soldier.

Hamish Macbeth felt like tearing his red hair out in frustration. Captain Davenport and Philomena Davenport were buried on the same day, in a little cemetery above Drim where seagulls screamed overhead. The sweep, poor Pete Ray, had already been buried in the churchyard at Lochdubh, his funeral being paid for by the locals.

Hamish attended the funeral, his eyes searching the small crowd of press and villagers for strangers, but he could see no one who looked suspicious or out of place. Strathbane police had vetted every member of the press. Milly was being supported by Ailsa. She seemed on the point of collapse.

Was she really so innocent? wondered Hamish. Did her sister-in-law simply leave saying she was going to Inverness and that was all? But Milly had been seen in the village all day when her sister had gone over the Struie Pass. The autopsy on what was left of Philomena's charred body had found traces of LSD, and so her death had been classed as murder.

He had a feeling that the murderer had not come all the way up from the south but was in Scotland somewhere. And he was sure it was someone who knew the Highlands well.

Whoever had attacked the captain had somehow managed to get him to walk out and meet
him and to go back with him to the house.

He longed to be able to go down to
Surrey himself but knew he would never get
permission.

Hamish decided to wait until things grew a
little quieter and then maybe take a holiday.

When the funerals were over and the villagers, all men – the women having decided to
honour the old tradition and not attend the
graveside – began to walk towards Milly's
house where refreshments were to be served,
Hamish caught up with Tam Tamworth.

'You seem to be getting close to Mrs
Davenport,' he said.

'Aye, she's a grand lady. She's promised me
a lot o' background exclusive after the murderer is found. But, to tell you, Hamish, I've a
bad feel about all this. Anyway, there's to be
no big Highland wake. It would be too much
for the poor woman. It's just going to be about
an hour of eats and drinks.'

'The locals won't like that. They'll be looking forward to their usual all-night fling.'

'Funny enough, they've got fond o' Milly
and knew a full Highland wake would upset
her so they're going along with it. Hey!
Who's this?'

A four-wheel drive had just drawn up outside the house as they approached it. Four
men got out dressed in sober black. 'If I'm not

mistaken,' said Hamish, 'that'll be the four old friends who he tricked out of money.'

'What! All the way from Surrey?'

'Maybe they're hoping to claw back some of the money from the widow.'

'At sich a time!' Tam strode forward. 'We'll see about that.'

Hamish hurried forward to catch Tam saying loudly, 'If you're that lot up from Surrey, I warn ye, now's not the time to be hassling the poor woman for money.'

Hamish pushed in front of Tam. 'I am investigating these murders,' he said, 'so I must ask each of you to identify yourselves.'

Ferdinand Castle introduced himself and then the others. Hamish studied them closely. Ferdinand was a tall, slight man with thinning hair and a bulbous nose. Thomas Bromley was small and tubby with a fat cheerful face. John Sanders was thin and wiry with a thick head of black hair and a clever face. Charles Prosser was straight-backed and military-looking with thick grey hair. All were expensively dressed, from their well-tailored coats and suits to their highly polished shoes.

'We are only here to pay our respects,' said Ferdinand. 'For all his faults, Captain Davenport was an old Army buddy. Where is Mrs Davenport?'

'Ben the hoose,' said Tam curtly. 'I suppose you'd better come in.'

Milly, wearing a simple black dress and looking very frail, was seated in an armchair at the window. She rose when the four men entered.

'How kind of you to come all this way,' she said. 'Did you bring your wives?'

'No, they all thought it too long a journey,' said John Sanders.

'Where are you staying?' asked Hamish.

'Over at the Tommel Castle Hotel. We booked in last night.'

'I know you have already made statements to the Surrey police,' said Hamish, 'but I'd like to call on you this evening just to get a beter idea about what sort of man Captain Davenport was.'

'Why?' demanded Charles Prosser.

'The more I can find out about the deceased, the better,' said Hamish. 'I am perfectly sure he went out on his last day to meet someone he knew.'

Thomas Bromley shrugged. 'If you think it will help.'

'Let's say six o'clock,' said Hamish.

The four looked at one another and then Ferdinand said curtly, 'Okay, but don't take all night over it.'

Hamish joined Jimmy, who was helping himself to a glass of whisky. 'Jimmy, can you e-mail me over the background on these four men?'

'Will do. But you're wasting your time. Solid alibis. Still, we're going to have a policewoman sleeping here tonight just to be on the safe side.'

After half an hour, the four visitors decided to go outside for a smoke. 'Well, would you just look at that,' said Ferdinand.

Hamish was helping Lugs down from the back of the police Land Rover while Sonsie jumped lightly to the ground on her large paws. 'Good heavens! The copper's got a couple of weird animals there,' said Thomas. 'A wild cat! And a dog with ears like Dumbo.'

'That policeman,' said Charles Prosser, 'looks like the village idiot, but what else can you expect in this arsehole of the world.'

Thomas Bromley shivered as he looked down to the long black finger of the loch and the steep, threatening black mountains that guarded it. 'At least the hotel's civilized. We'll say something nice to Milly and get going.'

'What about our money?' demanded Ferdinand.

'We'll wait a day. Call tomorrow and chat. Suggest she honours her husband's debts.'

News presenter Elspeth Grant was seated in the conference room at the television studios in Glasgow. The head of news and current affairs, Sean Gibb, said, 'We're going to launch this new programme we've been discussing called *Pandora's Box*. It's a sort of cold-case file. For the first programme, we want you to take some time up in the Highlands and see what you can dig up about those murders in Drim.'

'It's not very cold yet,' said Elspeth. 'And who will present the news while I'm away?'

'Dottie McDougal.'

'But Dottie's only a research assistant!'

'We've tried her out and she'll do great. She'll only be filling in until you see if you can make something of this idea. It's prime time, Elspeth.'

Elspeth felt very low. Dottie had blonde hair and cleavage. Dottie giggled and swayed her saucy little bum up and down the corridors. *Whoever believed that news presenters weren't chosen for their appearance?* she thought dismally.

'Why call it *Pandora's Box*?' she asked.

'Well, the last thing out of the box after all the horrors once Pandora had opened it was Hope. Get it? Captain Davenport's poor wifie wants closure, and that's the hope we're going to give her.'

Elspeth gamely made one last try. 'But I'm not a detective.'

'Look at all the cases you've been involved in up there. What's the name of that copper?'

'Hamish Macbeth,' said Elspeth bleakly.

'That's the fellow. Get alongside him.'

Elspeth repressed a sigh. The last time she saw Hamish was when he had tried to speak to her in Glasgow after she had fled their holiday in Corsica, convinced that he had proposed marriage to the love of his life, Priscilla Halburton-Smythe, whose father owned the Tommel Castle Hotel – and all because she had followed him and heard him asking about engagement rings. But there had been no news of any engagement in the newspapers, and she often wondered if Hamish had meant to propose to her.

Hamish had already phoned the manager, Mr Johnson, to see if he could beg a room to use for interviews. He was told he could use Colonel Halburton-Smythe's study as the colonel was away, visiting friends.

He decided to bring the four men in together. They had already been interviewed separately in Surrey.

Hamish sat behind the colonel's desk, and the four filed in and sat facing him. 'I'll start with you, Mr Castle,' said Hamish in his lilting Highland voice. 'I suppose you all met up in the regiment.'

'Yes, we went through some rough times. We were all in the Falklands War, and all of us served in Northern Ireland.'

'And you were all close to Captain Davenport?'

'Yes,' said Charles. 'Get on with it. We don't want to sit here answering questions all night.'

'Ah, Mr Prosser, what was your rank when you left the Army.'

'Colonel.'

'Mr Bromley?'

'Lieutenant-colonel.'

'Mr Castle?'

'Major.'

'And Mr Sanders?'

'Staff Sergeant.'

'Was Captain Davenport a good soldier?'

There was a chorus of agreement. 'The best.' Bromley. 'Fine fellow.' Castle. 'Good fun.' Sanders. 'Could always be relied on in a fix.' Prosser.

Hamish looked at them all thoughtfully. Then he said, 'Oh, come off it. We have letters from your lawyers, as you know, wanting your money back. I think he fled up here to get away from all the people he had conned. Someone wanted revenge. So let's get to the truth. Mr Davenport left the Army after long service with only the rank of captain. Why was that?'

John Sanders began to bluster. 'Who can explain the ways of the Army? I was only a sergeant, and—'

Charles Prosser cut in. 'May as well tell him. Nothing was ever proved but it left a nasty smell. It was when we were billeted in Northern Ireland. Someone sent an anonymous letter to the authorities saying that John here and Henry Davenport were selling arms to the IRA. Nonsense, of course. But mud sticks.'

Another problem, thought Hamish wearily. If it was true, and the captain had maybe taken money from the IRA and then not delivered, he would be a marked man. 'When was this supposed to have taken place?' he asked.

'Can't quite remember,' said John.

'Oh, tell the truth,' snapped Hamish, 'before I start digging up your records in Northern Ireland.'

'Nineteen eighty-six, I think,' said John sulkily. That pretty much rules out the IRA, thought Hamish. Davenport, before he fled north, had been living openly in Guildford. They'd have shot him by now.

'You all seem to have alibis for the time of Davenport's death, but can you think of any other old Army buddy he might have conned out of money?'

General shaking of heads. 'We five were always close,' said Charles. 'Now, look here, Officer, we've had a long journey and we're tired and want dinner.'

'I'll be seeing you again.'

As Hamish went out to the car park, he saw with a jolt at his heart the familiar figure of Elspeth getting out of a television van while a soundman and cameraman unloaded stuff from the back. A small, anxious-looking girl was dithering about.

'What's this?' exclaimed Hamish. 'Never say they've put you back to reporting.'

'Take me inside and buy me a drink and I'll give you the whole sad story. I'm weary. I've been travelling all day,' said Elspeth.

'I'd better see if my animals are all right.'

'For heaven's sake, Hamish. Can't they look after themselves for a moment?'

'No,' said Hamish curtly. He checked on Sonsie and Lugs, then walked with Elspeth into the hotel bar.

Hamish listened to Elspeth as she poured out her worries about the new programme, *Pandora's Box*, and her fears that the blonde would take away her news-presenting job.

'I wish you could solve this one quickly, Hamish,' she said.

'It's going to be difficult. There are four men here, friends of Captain Davenport, and they all have alibis.'

'Tell me about the case.'

Hamish settled back in his chair, gathered his thoughts, and told her everything he knew.

'Look,' said Elspeth, 'it's bound to be one of those four.' Her odd silver eyes gleamed with excitement.

'Why?'

'They must have hated him for diddling

them out of their money and yet they turn up for his funeral.'

'I've thought of that. I'm going over to Drim early to wait. If I'm not mistaken, they'll wait until they think Mrs Davenport is alone and then tell her she owes them the money. When she says she hasn't got it, they'll tell her to sell the house and divide up the proceeds amongst them.'

'Would they be so hard-hearted, right after the funeral?'

'I think so. I want to go back to the police station and go over their alibis. Jimmy has sent them over. There might be something there. If only I could go to Guildford and snoop around.'

'I might go to Guildford for you. But for now, I'll go with you to Drim. Two sets of eyes are better than one.'

Hamish shifted awkwardly. 'Like old times. Look, Elspeth, about Corsica . . .'

'Oh, never mind that. Let's go.'

In the police station, Hamish printed off the alibis. 'I'll take Castle and Bromley and you take Sanders and Prosser.'

Ferdinand Castle, he read, ran a small electronics firm that he had inherited on the death of his father. He had been seen by staff all day in his office; in the evening, he and his wife had dined at a local restaurant. Loads of witnesses.

In fact all of them had dined at the restaurant. Thomas Bromley and his wife had invited John Sanders and his wife, Charles Prosser and Mrs Prosser, along with the Castles, for dinner on the evening of the day of the murder. Thomas Bromley ran a chain of men's clothing stores, John Sanders repaired computers, and Charles Prosser ran a chain of supermarkets.

'Read about the dinner party?' he asked Elspeth. 'They could be covering for one another.'

'Yes, I thought of that, but John Sanders's neighbours reported all the comings and goings.'

'I wonder about that dinner party. I wonder if they got another old Army buddy who looks like one of them to stand in. Now, apart from Castle, one of the others could have taken a flight up to Glasgow, hired a car, and driven up there, then back again late the next day. That's what's missing. What were they all doing the day after? Whoever it was would need time to cover his tracks.'

'I was promised unlimited expenses to get this show on the road,' said Elspeth. 'What if I take my team over after I see them leave the hotel and film them coming out? Then I could go down to Guildford and start to dig.'

'Elspeth! That could be verra dangerous. One of them or all of them are psychopaths. If

Davenport had just been shot . . . but to stuff him up his own chimney and then attack the poor sweep.'

'It's very hard to get at me with a big television van, a soundman, a cameraman, and a wee researcher.'

'You have a researcher! She could be a help.'

'Betty Close is a wimp. She works hard but never seems to come up with anything useful. She'll need to come with us.'

'Maybe she can do some foot slogging. Send her out to the regiment's headquarters and see if she can dig up anything out there.'

'Maybe. Drive me back to the hotel, Hamish. I could do with a rest.'

'Could you tip me off when you see them leave?'

'Will do.'

'Oh, Elspeth, I've been meaning to explain about Corsica . . .'

'Another time. I'm too weary.'

She went out and shut the door behind her.

At least I'm not that attracted to her now, thought Hamish with a feeling of relief. But he remembered Elspeth when she used to work on the *Highland Times*: Elspeth with her charity-shop clothes and frizzy hair and those big grey eyes that turned silver, gypsy eyes, and he felt a little pang. The new Elspeth was sophisticated, and there was a hardness about her.

Chapter Four

I would like to be there, were it but to see
how the cat jumps.

— SIR WALTER SCOTT

The following morning, Hamish drove to Drim. Milly nervously called through the door, 'Who is it?'

'Hamish Macbeth.'

He had to wait until locks were opened and a chain removed.

'You're getting well protected,' he said, taking off his cap and following her into the kitchen.

'The villagers are so kind. There's a retired locksmith here and he came and put new locks all over the place, even on the windows.'

'Grand. Now, the reason I am here is because I think those four men will be back this morning, seeing if they can get any money out of you.'

'Right after the funerals! Surely not.'

'We'll see. Could you take them into the

drawing room and then I'll listen at the door to make sure you're all right?'

'I've known them all before,' said Milly, 'and their wives. We were all such friends.'

'Nonetheless, it's better to be safe. I hear the sound of a car. I'll wait in here until they're all safely in the drawing room.'

There was a knock at the door. Hamish listened hard. He could hear Milly welcoming the men. He waited until the voices went into the drawing room and he heard Milly shut the door. Then he nipped across the hall and pressed his ear to the panels.

They sat around at first, murmuring the usual platitudes about how sad and peculiar the death of Captain Davenport had been.

Then Thomas Bromley said in a coaxing voice: 'The sad thing is, Milly, that Henry owed us all money. We are sure you are going to honour your dead husband's debts.'

'It's an awful lot of money,' quavered Milly, 'and I don't have that much left.'

'Then you'll need to sell this house,' said John Sanders. 'I am sure you would not want people to think badly of your husband.'

Enough, thought Hamish. He pushed open the door and went in. 'Good morning, gentlemen,' he said. 'What is the reason for this call?'

'Just to give the lady our condolences.'

'It's too soon after all the shocks for Mrs

Davenport to be disturbed. I'll just be seeing you out.'

Hamish suddenly sensed evil in the room, but he did not know which one of them was emanating it.

He held the drawing-room door wide. 'Good day to you.'

Charles Prosser said haughtily, 'We'll be back to see you when this interfering policeman is not around.'

'No, you won't,' said Milly, getting to her feet. 'I've had enough. Don't come back. I haven't any money.'

'What's this?' asked Hamish. 'Have you been harassing Mrs Davenport for money at such a time?'

'We'll be on our way,' said Bromley. They pushed past Hamish and left.

Milly sobbed quietly while the sound of their car died away. 'Look here,' said Hamish, 'that money was got from them by fraud. You are not responsible.'

'I was thinking of selling the house,' said Milly, drying her eyes. 'But the village people are so kind. I've never really had friends of my own since I got married. To tell the truth, I didn't like their wives, but Henry insisted they were my best friends.'

'Will your sister-in-law have left you anything in her will?'

'I very much doubt it.'

Hamish took out his phone. 'I think I'll just be calling in a few favours from a couple of men on the Forestry Commission. As soon as all the shrubbery is taken away, you'll get a clear view of who's approaching the house.'

There was a knock at the door, and Milly winced. Hamish went to answer it. But it was Ailsa and Edie bearing a cake. 'We thought a bit o' cake might cheer her up.'

Milly appeared behind Hamish. 'How kind of you. Let's go into the kitchen. The drawing room is cold.'

Hamish returned to his phone call. 'Two forestry men'll be along this afternoon,' he said.

'What do I pay them?' asked Milly.

'Nothing. Like I said, they'll take away the wood as payment.'

When Hamish arrived back at his police station, he phoned the hotel and found to his dismay that none of the four had checked out. For once he would have welcomed Detective Inspector Blair with his bullying ways. Why wasn't he up at the hotel grilling them?

He phoned Jimmy and asked. 'I'm on my road over,' said Jimmy. 'Blair smells that this is a case that'll never be solved. He's got a glowing report on all four men from the regiment. He says I've got to concentrate on the villagers in Drim. He says they're probably all inbred and daft. He says some lunatic stuffed the captain up the chimney. He says we cannot go around annoying brave soldiers.'

'Ex-soldiers,' corrected Hamish, 'and they were up at Drim this morning, trying to get money out o' Milly.'

'Where are they now?'

'Tommel Castle.'

'I'll just be having a wee word wi' them.'

'Drop in here first. I've got an idea.'

When Jimmy arrived, demanding whisky as usual, Hamish said, 'Has anyone looked into how their businesses are doing?'

'Don't think so.'

'All of them or one of them must be desperate for money or they wouldn't go to such lengths.'

'I'll use your phone and get on to it. Where's Elspeth? I heard she'd been spotted.'

'Down in Surrey, trying to get some background.'

'Good luck to her. But believe me, the police down there have been thorough. Wait! I'll use your phone and get on to them and see if one of the four has a failing business.'

Hamish waited. The wind was rising like a bad omen. It had a peculiar keening sound, heralding worse to come.

* * *

Ailsa, Edie and Milly were eating cake and drinking coffee when someone knocked at the door. 'I'll go,' said Ailsa.

After a few minutes, she called, 'It's that reporter, Tam Tamworth.'

'Oh, show him in,' said Milly.

'Are you sure you want to be speaking to the press?' asked Ailsa.

'Tam swears he won't publish anything until the murders are solved. And he's kind.'

Ailsa ushered Tam into the kitchen. He was carrying a bunch of yellow roses, which he presented to Milly. 'How lovely, Tam. I'll put these in water.'

Ailsa winked at Edie, and both women rose to their feet. 'We'll leave you to it, Milly. Phone if there's anything you want.'

After they had gone, Tam nervously cleared his throat and said, 'It's my day off.'

'Then how nice of you to come to see me.'

'I wondered if you felt like a trip to Strathbane this evening for dinner.'

'Oh . . . I don't know. Wouldn't it look odd so soon after the funeral?'

'I don't think anyone will notice us. It just crossed my mind that it might be a wee bit o' a tonic to get out o' here. And you did want to see a film.'

'Oh, it would. Coffee?'

'I'll be on my way and pick ye up at seven o'clock.'

* * *

Jimmy came back from his phone call. 'Dead end. Yes, they investigated their finances and all are well off.'

'It's because they've been conned out of the money,' said Hamish slowly. 'The captain made a fool of them. I'll swear to God one of them hated him violently and the others are covering up.'

Elspeth was feeling she had made a wasted journey. She had hit a brick wall everywhere she went. The four men were considered model citizens. Not one of them had a dishonourable discharge from the Army. When she had tried to pump the adjutant about the captain's suspected selling of arms in Northern Ireland, she was told roundly that it had all turned out to be nonsense. Her researcher, Betty Close, worked hard and seemed eager but there was something about the girl that Elspeth did not like. Betty was small and sallow with a little beaky nose and a small mouth. Her one beauty lay in her eyes, which were large and dark brown, fringed with heavy lashes. She dyed her long hair black and had an irritating habit of tossing it around as if advertising shampoo.

Betty wanted Elspeth's job. She wanted everything that Elspeth had, from her flat down by the River Clyde to her status at the television station.

She knew Elspeth was worried about losing her job as a news presenter. Betty had over-heard the head of news and current affairs saying that if Elspeth could make anything of the *Pandora's Box* programme, then she would be an even bigger star. But she did not tell Elspeth this, constantly commiserating with her over the 'loss' of her presenting job. To which Elspeth always snapped back that she had not lost it.

'So are we back off up to peasant land?' asked the soundman, Phil Green.

'Not yet. I want to go via London. I've got to see an old friend in the City. I wonder if these four men are as successful in business as they claim. Why are they so desperate to get their money back? Is it just because they were conned?'

'London it is,' said the cameraman, George Lennox, gloomily.

The four men waited a couple of days before venturing to visit Milly again. As they approached, they saw that all the shrubbery in front of the house had been cleared away so that anyone approaching from any angle could be clearly seen.

They got down from their vehicle and rang the bell. Ailsa Kennedy answered the door. 'Whit?' she demanded.

'We are here to call on Mrs Davenport.'

'If you want money out o' her, forget it. We've phoned thae lawyers and you've no' got one damn thing in writing to say you ever lent him the money. You'll not come here again, pestering the poor woman.'

Her place was taken by a large man with big ears. 'I'm Tam Tamworth from the *Strathbane Journal*,' he said. 'This could be an interesting wee story for me. Are you all so broke that you're all the way up here harassing a widow woman?'

'You write one word and we'll sue!' said Charles Prosser.

'Go ahead.' Tam grinned. 'You cannae stop me writing about your bothering the widow, now, can ye? Get lost.'

The four men looked at him. For one brief moment, Tam felt a spasm of fear. They looked strong and menacing.

'This was just a friendly call before we leave,' said Charles Prosser smoothly.

'Oh, aye? So leave.'

As they walked back to their vehicle, Tam decided to watch his back in future. If one of that lot was a murderer, someone who had murdered two men viciously, and then a woman, too, he would not hesitate at another.

By the time she got back to the Tommel Castle Hotel, Elspeth had a raging temperature. To her dismay, Dr Brodie diagnosed swine flu and she was quarantined in her room. She tossed and turned, sometimes fretting over her job, sometimes wondering what had happened to the Highland Elspeth of old who reported happily on flower shows and sheep sales for the *Highland Times* and was not eaten up with ambition.

Betty Close saw her chance. She would see what information she could get out of Hamish Macbeth and send a preliminary report to Glasgow. And perhaps it was one of the locals who had committed the murders.

She decided to walk down to the village. If she told George or Phil what she was up to, they might tell Elspeth. Not that anyone was allowed in her room except Dr Brodie, who said he was sure he was immune to germs by now. But they could slip notes to her under the door. They had both done that already, wishing her a speedy recovery.

She met the manager, Mr Johnson, on her way out. 'And where are you off to?' he asked.

'Just going for a walk. I'll maybe pick up some background for Elspeth.'

'I should think Miss Grant knows all the village background, but you could try the seer, Angus Macdonald. He picks up a lot of gossip.' He gave her directions. 'Oh, you'd best drop by at Patel's grocery store and take him a present. He aye expects something.'

Betty walked out into the clear swimming light of a late-spring morning. What a peculiar place to live, she thought as she walked down to the village, stopping briefly on the hump-backed bridge over the River Anstey. The peaty river was swollen with the melting snow from the mountains above. The loch was very still and clear away from the place where the river waters tumbled into it. The village had been built as a result of the Highland clear-ances when the crofters had been driven off their land to make way for vast herds of sheep. Apart from a few Victorian villas and some council houses, the rest of the buildings were Georgian cottages, whitewashed and pretty. By the harbour was a large crumbling building that had once been a hotel. No one wanted to buy it so it lay abandoned, its empty windows staring out over the sea loch.

Betty walked into the grocery store. There were several women gossiping at the counter with the owner, but they fell silent when she entered. A large tweedy woman stepped for-ward. 'I am Mrs Wellington, the minister's wife.'

'Betty Close,' said Betty. 'I'm here with Elspeth Grant.'

'How is poor Miss Grant?'

'Still quite ill.'

'You must let us know when she is well enough to receive visitors. May we expect to see you at church this Sunday?'

'Sure,' said Betty, who had no intention of going.

Two small women looking exactly alike, from their rigidly permed white hair to their thick spectacles and camel-hair coats, stepped forward. 'We are the Misses Currie,' said Nessie. 'Do you need anything?'

'Need anything?' echoed the Greek chorus that was her sister, Jessie.

'As Miss Grant is unwell,' said Betty importantly, 'and we are here to research the murders, I am taking over. Do you think the murderer could be local?'

Frosty eyes looked at her, and the women turned away.

Betty shrugged and looked through the items in the small supermarket until she found a discounted box of biscuits. When she went back to the counter, the women had gone. She paid for the biscuits, walked out of the shop, and set off in the direction of Angus Macdonald's cottage.

She felt tired when she finally got there. It had been a long walk from the hotel, and Angus's cottage was perched on top of a steep brae.

She knocked at the door. A tall old man with a long grey beard opened the door and stared down at her. 'Come ben,' he said abruptly. 'You will be thon lassie who is a sidekick to our Elspeth.'

'I'm in charge now,' said Betty importantly. She looked around curiously, at the peat fire in the hearth with a blackened kettle hung over it on a chain, at the Orkney chairs on one side of the hearth and the battered wing chair on the other.

She handed Angus the box of biscuits. 'Cut price at Patel's,' he said. 'I thocht you lot would have had better expenses.'

Betty's sallow face coloured up in embarrassment. 'Sit down,' commanded Angus.

Betty made to sit down in the wing chair but Angus said, 'That's mine,' so she sat down on one of the Orkney chairs while he settled down and surveyed her with a gleam of amusement in his eyes.

'So you want to take Elspeth's job away from her,' commented Angus.

'Not at all. I am making enquiries because she is ill.'

'I wouldnae pin your hopes on her being out o' commission for long,' said Angus. 'The swine flu comes bad but it can be quite short and she's a healthy lass.'

'I've heard you see things,' said Betty gamely. 'I think maybe we're looking in the wrong place and the murders might have been committed by someone local.'

Angus studied her for a long moment. She wondered uneasily what he was thinking. Angus was not thinking about Betty. He was thinking maliciously about Hamish Macbeth.

He had overheard a tourist last summer asking about the 'famous seer' and heard Hamish say with a laugh, 'I think he relies more on local gossip than second sight.'

Angus was vain and had the Highland habit of plotting revenge long after the event.

'Now, Elspeth got a lot of her information up here before,' he said, 'from Hamish Macbeth. Very keen on Hamish is our Elspeth. We all thought at one time that they'd get married, but, och, he kept backing off. Don't interfere there, my girl, or you'll really hurt Elspeth and she would not like you getting information that would put her in the shade.'

'I would do nothing to hurt Elspeth,' said Betty. 'I must be on my way.'

Aye, and straight from here to the police station, thought Angus cynically.

He watched from the window as she hurried down the brae, and then he clutched at the sill. It seemed as if a dark shadow was creeping across the heather to engulf her. He shook his head and the vision disappeared.

But Hamish Macbeth was not at his police station. He was on his road to Inverness. He thought not enough had been done to investigate the woman who had helped to abduct Philomena.

He drove into the car park of the Dancing Scotsman, went into the bar, and asked to speak to the waitress who had previously been interviewed by the police. A plump waitress came forward wearing her uniform of frilly white blouse and Buchanan tartan pinafore dress.

'I'm sure I cannae tell ye more than I've already told the police afore,' she said.

'Maybe we could just sit down and have a wee chat,' suggested Hamish. The waitress, whose name was Rose Cameron, looked around the near-empty bar.

'Won't do any harm. It's fair quiet.'

'I know you've been through all this before and I've read the reports. But if you could just be describing her to me again.'

Hamish was in plain clothes and was driving an old car borrowed from the garage in Lochdubh, not wanting to alert Inverness police that he was poaching on their patch.

Rose was quite old for the job. Her face was wrinkled, and her sagging mouth showed that she had lost all her teeth some time ago. 'Let's see,' she said. 'She was a bit on the fat side, dressed in a suede jacket and trousers. Her hair was hidden under one of those tweed fishing hats.'

'Face?'

'Roundish. Maybe she'd been to the dentist because she had a wee bittie difficulty speaking, as if her mouth was still frozen.'

'What kind of accent?'

'Posh. Lowlands. She came up to the bar for her first drink afore she joined that dead woman and I heard her telling the barman she was from Edinburgh.'

Hamish brightened. He now had one fact that the police had missed.

'And she didn't pay by credit card?'

'No, cash. We were busy at the time so I didn't take much notice.'

'Did the Inverness police examine the tape from the security cameras?'

'They tried. But the boss is a bit mean ower small things and there wasn't any tape in there.'

'She surely wasn't wearing gloves. There must have been some fingerprints.'

'By the time they got around to asking, her glass had been washed and the table she sat at wiped clean.'

Hamish asked a few more questions and then returned to his hired car, deep in thought. Would a ruthless murderer want a woman around who could identify him? Maybe blackmail him?

The wives of his four suspects were all in Guildford at the time of Philomena's abduction and murder with plenty of witnesses. He frowned as he remembered the police reports.

The four men had pretty much alibied one another. But it would take only one of them to be the murderer with his mates covering up for him.

He drove back to Lochdubh as fast as the old banger of a car he had rented would let him.

Sonsie and Lugs were waiting outside the police station for him. He had forgotten to feed them before he left but he was pretty sure the pair of them would have gone along to the kitchen door of the Italian restaurant, where the staff spoiled them. They could come and go by a large cat flap in the kitchen door of the police station.

'They've been fed,' said a voice behind him.

He swung round. Angela Brodie, the doctor's wife, stood there, her soft wispy hair blowing around her thin face. 'They were eating like pigs outside the Italian restaurant. Lugs is particularly fond of osso buco.'

'I'll make us some coffee,' said Hamish.

'How's the case going?' asked Angela when they were seated at the kitchen table.

'Not well.'

'Been to see Elspeth? She'll soon be past the infectious stage.'

'I'll head up there later. What should I take her?'

'I think she would like something easy to read.'

'I'll look for something. I'd better check that those four bastards have left the area.'

'Do you suspect one of them?'

'Yes, I do.'

'But why? I gather Davenport owed them all money, but they all seem to be pretty well off.'

'I think I'm dealing with a psychopath with an overweening vanity.'

When Angela had left, Hamish went through to the police office and called Jimmy Anderson.

'Jimmy, this is one hell of a long shot. It's about that woman who helped our murderer abduct Philomena.'

'What about her?'

'I think she was in disguise.'

'Stands to reason.'

'I mean I think she had stuffed her face and body to make herself look fatter. The waitress said she spoke as if she'd just been to the dentist. And she said she was from Edinburgh.'

'What are you getting at?'

'Could you do me a favour? Could you get on to Edinburgh police and give them, say, the day after Philomena's murder, or the day after that, and ask if there were any suspicious deaths in Edinburgh?'

'The damn city's probably got a long list. Okay, I'll let you know.'

'I'm going out to take my beasts for a walk.'

'Hamish, I probably won't get back to you until this evening.'

'I'll be waiting.'

Hamish put down the phone. He felt a draught on the back of his neck and went into the kitchen. The door was slightly open. He frowned. He was sure he had shut it. Sonsie and Lugs were nowhere in sight. He decided to go out and look for them. He locked the kitchen door, put the key up in the gutter above the door, and set off.

Betty crept out from behind the henhouse, where she had fled when she heard Hamish put down the phone.

She quickly nipped up to the kitchen door, took the key down from the gutter, and let herself in.

Inside the police-station office, Betty took a small, powerful tape recorder out of her bag and searched for a place to hide it. There was a shelf of files above the desk. She set it up there and let herself out, heading off up the back way, through Hamish's grazing flock of sheep, and made her way by a roundabout route back to the hotel.

She had read about Hamish in the Glasgow office. With any luck he might be on to something and she could steal the show from Elspeth.

Hamish found Lugs and Sonsie along the waterfront, took them back to the police station, and loaded them into the Land Rover. He collected a pile of old paperbacks and headed off for the Tommel Castle Hotel.

He was met by Dr Brodie, who told him that it might be an idea to leave Elspeth alone for another couple of days, although she appeared to be much better. Hamish handed him the pile of books and asked him to take them up to her.

He drove off towards the police station. Rain was smearing the windscreen. For once the wind of Sutherland had deserted the county. The waters of the loch lay still and dark, and the pine forest opposite was obscured by mist.

He parked at the police station. Lugs and Sonsie followed him in. Lugs gave a sharp bark, and the fur on Sonsie's back was raised. Hamish stood inside the door, listening, waiting, and sniffing the air. There was a faint smell of perfume. He went back out to the Land Rover and collected his forensic kit. He sprinkled powder on the entrance to the kitchen and then carefully dusted it. Footprints. Not his. Small and neat. He sat back on his heels. He went to the police-station office on his knees, powdering and dusting as he went. The footprints stopped in front of his desk. He fingerprinted in his office until he found the powerful little tape recorder hidden behind the files. Hamish carefully fingerprinted it as well. He went out and back to the waterfront. Toddling through the mist came the Currie sisters.

'Nice soft day,' said Nessie.

'Soft day,' murmured her sister.

'Press been bothering you?' asked Hamish.

'They've mostly gone,' said Nessie.

'Gone,' echoed Jessie dolefully.

'Excepting that wee lassie, her that came up wi' Elspeth,' said Nessie as Hamish tuned out the echo that was Jessie. 'I think she tried to call on you but you were away. I saw her near the police station.'

Hamish returned to the station. Putting on a pair of latex gloves, he turned on the recorder, listened to the noise of his search, and erased it. Then he put the recorder on his desk, dialled Strathbane headquarters, and cut off the call before anyone could answer so that there would only be the sound on the tape recorder of the dialling beeps. He pretended to be speaking to Jimmy Anderson. 'Jimmy, this is Hamish,' he said, his voice full of excitement. 'I think I've got our man. He's camping on the beach at Durness. I'm off up there for a recce. Don't send the troops yet, I'll phone you from there.'

He turned to his pets, who were studying him.

'Come along. I know ye don't like the siren but we're going to blast out o' this village.'

On the waterfront, Betty swung round as Hamish's Land Rover sped past with the siren going and the lights flashing. She made her way by a roundabout route to the police station. Once inside, she eased the tape recorder out from behind the files where Hamish had replaced it and switched it on. Her eyes grew

wide with excitement. She went out quickly
up to the back fields and called the soundman
and the cameraman. 'Big break on the story,'
she said. 'Pick me up in Lochdubh. I'll be outside the shop on the waterfront.'

'We'll tell Elspeth,' said George Lennox, the
cameraman.

'Don't do that,' said Betty quickly. 'She's too
ill. May come to nothing.'

She went to Patel's grocery store and waited
impatiently outside until the large television
Winnebago hove into view.

Hamish, hiding in a lay-by behind a stand of
trees, watched the Winnebago rush by, heading north.

The television team stopped overnight at a
small hotel and started out again at dawn.
Betty's heart rose as the weather changed. The
wind rose from the west, driving away the rain
and mist until the blue sky arched above.
George Lennox was driving. He was rather
surly in the way of some TV cameramen.
Perhaps it was understandable, as the presenter on any programme got all the glory, no
matter how dangerous the situation. Phil
Green was small and cheerful and kept
exclaiming at the beauty of the landscape. Up
and down the narrow roads they went until at
long last they drove into Durness and down to

where a curve of pure white sand faced a green-and-blue sea.

There was no sign of any police Land Rover. Betty climbed stiffly down. It was still and quiet apart from the ceaseless sound of the sea.

She had a sudden queasy feeling of unease. 'This is grand,' said Phil. He had a thermos and a pack of sandwiches. He sat down on a flat rock and stared dreamily out to sea. 'This is God's country!'

'This is the bloody end o' the world that God forgot,' said George, glaring at Betty. 'Are you sure o' this? There's nobody camping on the beach.'

'We'll just need to search around,' said Betty desperately.

'You go and search,' said Phil lazily. 'Me, I'm staying right here until you find something.'

Betty scrambled up from the beach. There were ruined croft houses here and there. No people. The wind whistled amongst the ruins, and the sad cry of a curlew from the heather seemed to mock her.

Elspeth was feeling much stronger. She sat up in bed and then saw a note, which had been pushed under her door. She struggled out of bed and picked it up.

'Dear Elspeth,' she read. 'Your wee researcher had the nerve to hide a tape recorder in my office so I sent her off on a wild goose chase to Durness. Get well soon. Hamish.'

Elspeth phoned the television station in Glasgow and asked for her boss. He listened in horror and then said, 'Get her back down here. When you're better, get back down yourself. We've had a lot of complaints about your replacement. And see if you can smooth over that bobby friend o' yours before he sues us.'

But Hamish had more to worry him now than one overambitious researcher. When he had returned earlier to the station, it was to find Angela Brodie waiting for him. 'I've come to confess,' she said seriously.

Chapter Five

> *To marry is to domesticate the Recording Angel. Once you are married, there is nothing left for you, not even suicide, but to be good.*
> — ROBERT LOUIS STEVENSON

When they were seated at the kitchen table, Hamish said, 'Not to the murders, I hope.'

Angela gave a miserable little attempt at a laugh. 'Not them.'

'Well, what?'

She took a deep breath. 'I gave money to Captain Davenport.'

Hamish's stomach gave a lurch. 'You what?'

'It happened like this. I didn't tell anyone. My last book was rejected. I felt I had lost my cards of identity. My agent said there was nothing up with the book, it was just that the publishers had paid out a vast sum to some celebrity and despite all the publicity, it was remaindered after a few weeks and they lost tons of money. So they turned to their list and started axing off authors who weren't big sellers.'

'So where on earth does the captain come into this?'

'I was upset and I went out for a very long walk and I came across the captain. I was very teary and he seemed kind. He asked me what was the matter and I told him. To my amazement, he said he could fix it for me. He knew a very good vanity press that would publish and publicize my book for five thousand pounds. Now, when I was nominated for the Haggart Prize, I got a large cheque for the publication of my last book. My husband and I have separate accounts. I never told him how much it was, and, oddly enough, he didn't ask. He just said he thought a new author would be lucky if they got more than a few hundred pounds and I said, "Yes, isn't it sad."'

'But why? I would have said Dr Brodie was an easy-going, generous man.'

'I know. But I wanted my independence. I didn't want to be just a housewife any more.'

'So you gave Davenport the money.'

Angela bowed her head, and a tear ran down her thin cheek.

'So what did you do?'

'I phoned him and he said it was all going ahead. Then I phoned after a few weeks and he said, "I never took any money from you and I don't even know who you are."'

'But Angela, the bank will have a record of your cheque.'

She shook her head dismally.

'Neffer say you paid the man in cash!'

She nodded, and then burst out with, 'What else was I to think except that he was thoroughly honest?'

'Did you call on him?'

'I tried. His wife answered the door. She looked scared but she said he wasn't at home even though the car was parked outside. Mind you, he often went for long walks, or so he told me.'

'Why didn't you say anything before? It looks right bad.'

'And be dragged off to Strathbane by Blair?'

Hamish sat back in his chair. She started to speak again, but Hamish said gently, 'Shh! I'm thinking.'

At last he said, 'Here's what we'll do. If you can wait until tomorrow, Elspeth should be ready for visitors. You tell her your story and get filmed. Then you let her drive you to police headquarters in Strathbane the following day after she's got her bit shown on the telly. No, they can't arrest you, but you'll have an unpleasant time of it. The others'll be waiting for you when you come out. Be brave. Tell them what drove you into giving the captain the money. Think o' the publicity! Might start a debate about literary authors getting axed because of vast sums paid to celebrities who can't even write. I think it might get you a publisher.'

'What will my husband say?'

'I'll talk to him. Have you any money left?'

'Yes.'

'So take my advice and get some of the village women in to clean your house. I'm sure Dr Brodie doesn't notice much but he'll be in a better mood wi' a bit o' home comfort.'

Betty trudged wearily back to the beach. She had tried to call her colleagues but could not pick up a signal on her phone. As she neared the beach, though, her phone worked at last and she called Phil Green. His voice crackled back over a bad line. 'I looked for you, Betty. Thon policeman sent you off on a wild goose chase. He says you planted a recorder in the police office. We've been told to go back and join Elspeth immediately. You're to make your own way back.'

'How?' screamed Betty, looking wildly around.

'Taxi.'

'*Here?*'

'Not my problem.' Phil rang off.

Dr Brodie was bewildered as Hamish explained the situation. When Hamish had finished, he asked plaintively, 'What's up with being just a housewife? The village is full of them.'

In a shaky voice, Angela explained how much it had meant to her to be a published writer.

'It's all beyond me, Angela,' he said at last. 'But you've been awfully secretive. Did you think I'd want your money?'

'No, no. It's just I've never had any money of my own. It felt great.'

Dr Brodie shook his head wearily. 'Och, do what you have to do.'

Betty arrived back the following day. She had stayed overnight at Balankiel, taken a bus to Lochinver, and from there travelled by taxi to Lochdubh. A curt message from the television station was waiting for her telling her to return immediately to Glasgow.

Elspeth, completely recovered, was down in Lochdubh, filming Angela, who was seated at her computer at a newly scrubbed and cleared kitchen table. After the filming was over, Hamish said urgently, 'Now, remember, Elspeth, I don't know anything about this.'

As Hamish walked back to his station, he suddenly stood stock-still. He had been focusing on the four men. What if Angela turned out not to be the only local who had parted with money? He had to see Milly again. He walked to the offices of the *Highland Times* and told Matthew Campbell, the editor, to get down to Strathbane because he'd just heard a rumour that Angela Brodie had been arrested. Then he went back to the police station to wait through the long day for the evening news.

At six o'clock, he switched on the Scottish television news. Floods here, road accidents there, murder in Glasgow. 'Come on,' he muttered.

And suddenly there was Angela outside Strathbane police headquarters, her eyes red with crying. Blair had been at his worst until Elspeth had demanded a lawyer for her.

Then it switched to Angela in her kitchen telling her sad story to Elspeth. Hamish breathed a sigh of relief. She came over very well. Angela exuded goodness.

Henry Satherwaite ran a small publishing firm in Edinburgh called simply, Scottish Literature. He published new authors and had built up a surprisingly successful business with steady sales. He had read Angela's first book and had thought it very good. He promptly packed an overnight bag, got his car out of the garage, and headed for the Highlands.

Jimmy Anderson called on Hamish that evening. 'Come ben,' said Hamish, eyeing him warily, hoping the foxy detective had not jumped to the same miserable conclusion as he had himself – that there might be more conned villagers in the neighbourhood.

'So your friend has got herself in hot water wi' Blair,' said Jimmy. He raised the glass of whisky Hamish had poured him and said, 'Rummel, rummel roon the gums, look out stomach here it comes. Ah, that's better.'

'It's your liver, not your stomach, you should be worried about.'

'Oh, I'm fine. But have you thought?'

'Thought what?'

'These con artists just keep on going. They jist can't keep their paws off other people's money. Your friend Angela Brodie might not be the only one.'

'Maybe,' said Hamish.

'Aye, I should guess definitely, which widens the investigation.'

'Have you suggested this to Blair?'

'Not yet.'

'Wait a bit.'

'Won't do, Hamish. Do you want me to go all telly on you and say, *I will give you twenty-four hours*? Sorry. I left a memo on the fat yin's desk.'

'I'd better get over to Drim in the morning.'

'Why not Lochdubh?'

'Who, for instance?'

'Could be anyone. He could ha' promised thae Currie sisters facelifts. I've dealt with fraudsters and cons before, Hamish, and it's amazing how easily people are tricked out of their money. Besides, the captain's wife said that he didn't mix wi' any of the folk from Drim.'

'Any murders in Edinburgh just after Philomena's?'

'Only one odd one. A brass nail fell out o' the window o' her flat in the Royal Mile to her death. Place went on fire.'

Correctly interpreting *brass nail* to mean 'prostitute', Hamish asked, 'Suspicious circumstances?'

'You could say that. Bruises on her ankles made it look as if someone had bent down and heaved her out. The fire was started at the fireplace.'

'Did she have a pimp?'

'No, she was an independent lady called Sarah Brogan.'

'It would be a good idea to give the Edinburgh police the photos of our four men and see if anyone in the tenement recognized one of them.'

'I suggested that and was told by Daviot to stop flying off at mad tangents.'

'I'll try to catch Elspeth,' said Hamish. 'I hope she hasn't left for Glasgow. She might look into it for me.'

'What about another dram?' asked Jimmy, raising his empty glass.

'Not when you're driving.'

'Calvinist,' said Jimmy. 'I'm off.'

Betty Close packed slowly. She was reluctant to leave. She wondered whether to plead with Elspeth to keep her job, because she had a nasty feeling she might be sacked when she returned to Glasgow.

She heard Hamish's voice along the hotel corridor. 'Might be a story for you, Elspeth.'

Betty waited until she heard the door of Elspeth's room close. She crept along the corridor and pressed her ear to the panels of Elspeth's door. She heard Hamish say, 'It's a long shot, but when Philomena left that bar, she left with a woman described as small and plump, but she wouldn't want to be recognized and could have padded herself with something and altered her appearance. The waitress said she seemed to have difficulty speaking, which might mean that her cheeks were padded with something to alter her face. Now, after Philomena's murder, a prostitute in the Canongate seems to have been shoved out of the tenement window of her flat and then the place was set on fire. Maybe you could get photos of our four suspects and ask if anyone saw one of them on the day she died.'

Betty heard Elspeth reply, 'I don't know if I'll have time to do anything, Hamish. It's such a long shot. I have to get back first and secure my job. Leave it with me.'

'What about that creature who put the tape recorder in the station?'

'Don't know. She's been summoned back to Glasgow. I've got her a plane ticket from Inverness. I can't bear the idea of her company on the road back. You'd better go,' said Elspeth. 'I've got a lot to do.'

Betty scuttled back along the corridor. She sat down in her room, engulfed with a sudden wave of hate for Elspeth. She would get over to Edinburgh as soon as she could and see if she alone could solve the murders.

Hamish went over to Drim in the morning, stopping only once to let the dog and cat out to play in the heather.

He then drove down into Drim and parked outside the shop. He sat for a moment looking at the gale whipping little whitecaps down the long black loch.

A dingy-looking black-headed gull stood at the edge of the water and surveyed him with contempt, then flew away.

Hamish climbed down from the Land Rover, opened the door of the shop, and went in. Jock Kennedy was behind the counter. 'Where's Ailsa?' asked Hamish.

'Up at the hoose. What do you want to be bothering her for?'

'Just a helpful gossip.'

'Oh, well, you know the way.'

Jock had knocked down an old fishing cottage at the back of the shop and replaced it with a rather awful pebble-dashed bungalow. The builders had not allowed for the fierce gales funnelled down the loch. The old cottage had stood side-on to them with very thick walls. The new building was on a little rise facing down the loch. Hamish clutched his cap and rang the bell.

Ailsa answered it and said, 'It's yourself. I've just put the kettle on.'

Hamish eased past her and walked into the kitchen. He noticed that despite the double-glazing on all the windows, little draughts were somehow escaping into the house. The kitchen was cold.

'Tea?'

'Aye, that would be grand,' said Hamish.

He waited until Ailsa made a pot of tea and put it on the table with two mugs. 'Now,' she said. 'What brings you?'

Ailsa was still a good-looking woman, Hamish noticed, with her thick red hair and creamy skin.

'Did you see that bit about Angela on the telly?' asked Hamish.

'Aye. Poor soul.'

'Well, it couldnae help but cross my mind that there might be other folk that the captain took money from.'

Ailsa's eyes became blank. 'Now, I would not be knowing about that.'

Hamish stared dreamily at the ceiling. 'I think when she sells the house, Mrs Davenport will be looking to pay back as much as she can. Now, if someone in Drim was feeling the pinch, and all because of that fraudster, wouldn't it be chust grand if that person knew he or she might be getting their money back?'

There was a long silence. The wind screeched around the house like a banshee.

Ailsa suddenly rose to her feet. 'I'm not saying anything, mind. But let's drop in on Edie.'

As they walked to Edie's home, Hamish remembered that when a charming young Englishman had caused a flutter amongst the hearts of the women of Drim, Edie had set up an exercise class in the village hall as they all tried to lose weight.

Edie answered the door to them. 'This is nice,' she said. 'Come ben.'

She led the way into a small, shabby living room. 'Nobody else dead, I hope?' she said.

'I wondered if you knew that Mrs Davenport plans to refund as much of the money as she can that her husband tricked people out of?' said Hamish, reflecting that he'd better go and see Milly afterwards and tell her about it.

'Go on,' said Ailsa softly. Edie was a thin, scrawny woman wearing a pink tracksuit. Hamish judged her to be somewhere in her sixties. She was heavily made-up, from mascara on her sparse eyelashes to bright red lipstick on her small drooping mouth. No teeth, thought Hamish. Dentures. Women of her generation often got all their teeth pulled out at an early age 'to get it over and done with', sometimes after only about two extractions. They never thought how their faces would begin to droop and how the shape of the mouth would be spoiled.

Edie's bony shoulders rose in a dismal little shrug. 'I've been a right fool. You remember, Hamish, when we had that murder here? Before that, I ran the exercise classes. It was all such fun and excitement. I was out for a walk one day and saw the captain up ahead of me. I thought I'd take him to task for not shopping at the village store. Thae supermarkets are killing off all the wee shops. It's a disgrace, that's what it is!'

'Yes, yes,' said Hamish soothingly. 'And then what happened?'

'He wasn't what I expected. He was awfy kind and polite. He said he would start to buy groceries at the shop. He said it must be a lonely life for a sophisticated lady like me. I found myself telling him about missing all the excitement I'd had when I ran the classes. Oh, he said, you should start an exercise salon in Strathbane. I said I hadn't the money. He said that he'd a friend in Strathbane who would back me if I put in a small down payment but it'd need to be in cash.

'I asked him how much and he said, one thousand pounds. Well, I just had that much and not much over in my post office savings account, but after we'd talked for a long time and I could practically *smell* that salon, I said all right. I'd call at his house with it. And I did. He told that wee wife of his to take a walk and leave us alone. He said to me that Milly was a bit of a fool and didn't understand business. I still hung on to the money in my bag, I was that nervous with the idea of parting with it. But, och, he gave me a couple of drinks and I've aye had a weak head and he *fed* my dreams. I gave him the money.

'After that, I called at the house a couple o' times but the wife always said he wasn't at home and she always looked as if she'd been crying. I watched and waited one day until I saw him marching off for one of his walks. I followed him. He denied the whole thing. I said I'd go to the police. He smiled and said, "What proof do you have? You'll just look like some senile old fool."'

'Did you tell Jock?' Hamish asked Ailsa.

She shook her head. 'Edie swore me to secrecy.'

Thank goodness for that, reflected Hamish. If word had got around what had happened to Edie, then he would have to suspect the village men, who would have banded together behind Jock to teach the captain a lesson.

'Will you be taking me in?' asked Edie. Tears were running down her thin face. Her mascara ran in black streaks.

'I'll keep it quiet for now,' said Hamish. 'I'll see what I can do.'

When he left, he looked down to the beach. Lugs and Sonsie were chasing each other around and seemed to be having a good time. He walked on up to Milly's house.

She led him into the kitchen, where he found Tam Tamworth ensconced by the stove. 'Get lost, Tam,' ordered Hamish. 'This is private business.'

'Anything that concerns Milly concerns me,' said Tam.

'Please, Tam,' said Milly. 'I must hear what he has to say.'

He closed the kitchen door behind him. Hamish waited a moment and then jerked the door back open. Tam nearly fell in. 'Out!' ordered Hamish. 'As far away as you can go.'

Tam gave a sheepish smile and walked to the front door. Hamish waited until he heard the door slam behind him and returned to Milly.

He told her about Edie Aubrey. 'But that's awful,' said Milly. 'I'll give you a cheque

107

for her. I've already sent a cheque to Angela Brodie.'

'I'm afraid there might be others. How are you situated financially?'

'I thought I had enough to keep me going for a bit and then I've got Henry's Army pension and my widow's pension. But if those four colleagues of Henry's are telling the truth, then I will need to sell this house.

'Oddly enough, ever since Henry's death, I've begun to like this place. The women are so friendly.'

'I wouldn't pay any more until the murder is solved. I mean, I don't trust those men. Any one of them or all of them could be claiming inflated amounts of money. What's Tam doing hanging around?'

'Oh, he's been so kind.'

'I'm warning you, a reporter will be kind to anyone to get a story.'

'Tam's not like that. He's promised to only write up any background I give him after the murder is solved.'

'Get it in writing,' said Hamish cynically.

'I'll get you that cheque,' said Milly in a thin little voice. She obviously did not like any criticism of Tam.

When she returned with the cheque, Hamish left and found Tam moodily kicking at a clod of earth in the garden.

'Don't you go messing up that poor woman,' cautioned Hamish.

'It's not like that,' said Tam. He turned dark red and gave the clod another kick. 'Fact is, I've got it bad. I want tae marry the lass.'

Hamish stared at him in amazement. They were in the lee of the house so he had heard clearly what Tam had said.

'Why?' he asked.

'She's such a lady wi' her gentle ways, and I've a mind to settle down.'

'She doesn't have much money.'

Hamish sidestepped quickly as Tam took a swipe at him. 'I love her, you useless loon!'

'All right, all right,' said Hamish, backing off. 'Invite me to the wedding.'

As Hamish walked back down towards the village, he turned and looked back. The bushes had all been cleared, and only the monkey puzzle tree remained. It meant that Milly would have a clear view of anyone approaching the house.

He gave a tearful and delighted Edie her cheque and then headed to the beach. Sonsie and Lugs were now sheltering beside the Land Rover. He noticed that the sea loch's tide was very high – higher than he could ever remember it.

He had an uneasy feeling that the seas were coming back to claim the land they had lost.

Chapter Six

The shadows now so long do grow,
That brambles like tall cedars show,
Molehills seem mountains, and the ant
Appears a monstrous elephant
— CHARLES COTTON

Betty Close did not lose her job because, when it came to grovelling, she could out-grovel Detective Inspector Blair. Instead, she was suspended for a month.

She decided to use her time off following up the death of the Edinburgh prostitute instead of moping in her flat in Glasgow. She got off at Waverley Station and made her way up the Mound to the Royal Mile.

People have been living in the Royal Mile for the last seven thousand years. It runs from the Castle to Holyrood Palace down the shoulder of a former volcano. Betty's grandmother had told her that when she was a child, she remembered the tall tenements on the Royal Mile containing some really dreadful slums. But restoration and cachet had turned the famous street into somewhere desirable to live.

Betty found the actual address, which she had discovered by trawling through back numbers of the Edinburgh papers. The death of Sarah Brogan had only qualified for a small paragraph in the *Scotsman*. The procurator fiscal had refused to pass a verdict of suicide, and it said the police were still investigating.

The tenement was up a close off the Canongate, a close being the narrow passage that led to the flats. She had brought with her still photographs of the four men. Betty started at the top flat where Sarah had lived. There was no police tape on the door. She pressed the bell, but nobody answered. There was no answer at the flat across the landing, either.

Betty tried a flat on the next floor down. The whole building seemed expensive and well maintained. She reflected that the late Sarah must have been very good at her job. This time someone did answer the door, a small thickset man with a balding head and small black eyes.

Betty showed him the photographs and asked if he recognized any of the men. She explained that she was investigating Sarah's death for a television documentary. He put on a pair of glasses and carefully studied the photographs.

'No, I can't say I recognize anyone,' he said at last. He had a voice that the Scots would describe as 'refeened', rather strangulated as he tried to imitate a 'posh' English accent.

'Can you think of anyone who lives here who might have known her?' asked Betty.

He shook his head. 'We keep ourselves to ourselves. The other residents are practically all out during the day. I'd suggest you come back sometime after six o'clock. It's a good thing the fire brigade were quick off the mark or I'd have lost my flat as well.'

She found that what he had said about the other residents being out during the day was true. She pressed bell after bell on her road down without success. She tried a few of the neighbouring shops and a café, still failing to find anyone who had known Sarah.

Betty passed the time by going down to Princes Street and looking at the shops. A true Glaswegian, she felt out of place in Edinburgh and found herself longing to get the train back to Glasgow. But just before six o'clock, she wearily trekked back to the Canongate and entered the close leading to the tenement. The aristocracy, she remembered, used to live in the Royal Mile but had deserted it in the eighteenth century to move to the New Town behind Princes Street. It was still daylight outside but the close was dark and the lamps had not been lit, no doubt as one of the new measures to leave lights off as long as possible to save energy.

There was a dark alcove in the close. Just as she was passing it, she received a smashing blow on the skull. She died instantly and did not feel the hands that shoved her small inert body into a large suitcase on wheels.

Betty had been an orphan and a menopause baby. She had no brothers or sisters, and the only relation she had known had been her mother's sister, who died the year before of cancer. And because she had been suspended for a month, no one noticed she was missing.

Her body in the suitcase loaded down with stones eventually lay at the bottom of a quiet stretch of the Gareloch in Argyll after being tipped over the side of a rowing boat.

Back in Lochdubh, Hamish was relieved to find that the four men had left, so there was no fear of Milly being bullied further. But now he had the weight of worry that the murderer might be one of the locals. He diligently went all over the area where the captain might have walked, talking to crofters, and then to every house in Drim but without any success.

Just to be sure, he checked up on Edie Aubrey. On the day of the captain's death, she had been seen with Ailsa. There was no indication that she had gone near the captain's home.

He wondered, as spring eased into a glorious early summer and bell heather began to bloom on the flanks of the towering mountains, whether this would be a case he would ever solve. He itched to go down to Guildford. He had holiday owing but felt reluctant to use up his dwindling bank balance on what could be a wild goose chase prompted by his desire to find a murderer outside of his beloved Sutherland.

One fine morning, he wandered out on to the waterfront and leaned on the wall overlooking the loch. The air was clean and fresh, scented with pine from the forest across the loch and with the more homely smells of frying bacon and baking scones. Angela Brodie came hurrying to join him.

'Hamish, I've just been correcting the proofs of my new book.'

'So that Edinburgh publisher's turned out all right?'

'Oh, he's great. I'm going down to Edinburgh to have lunch with him tomorrow. How's the case going?'

'I cannae get anywhere, Angela, and that iss a fact,' said Hamish, the strengthening of his accent showing that he was upset. 'I fear it's going to turn out to be one of the locals. You weren't the only one.'

'Who . . . ?'

115

'I cannae be saying. I feel like taking time off and going down to Guildford but I'm a bittie stretched at the bank.'

'Milly gave me back that money, so I could give you some.'

'No, I couldn't be taking it. I want to be able to enjoy a grand day like this without the shadow of those damn murders hanging over the place. Who else goes for long walks?'

'Not many of us. You know what it's like in the country. Some of them at the end of the waterfront even drive their cars along to Patel's. Oh, I know. I've thought of someone. Do you remember Effie Garrard?'

'Of course. The one that was murdered and had pretended to be an artist when it turned out to be her sister's work.'

'Well, the sister, Caro, spent some of the winter down in Brighton but she's back. She's had that awful corrugated iron roof taken off and a good slate one put on instead. I heard she likes to go for long walks.'

'I'll try her.' Hamish sighed. 'I'm at a dead end anyway. Tell me, Angela, I never asked. You're no fool. What was there about the captain that made you believe him?'

'I suppose he had the professional fraudster's gift of finding out people's dreams and playing on them. I felt hurt, rejected by my old publisher. He was so easy to talk to. I hear how he treated his poor wife like dirt but he made you feel you were the most important person in the world.'

Hamish was once more amazed that Caro Garrard had decided to keep the cottage in the Highlands that had once belonged to her murdered sister.* The new slate roof gleamed in the sunlight, and the walls had been newly whitewashed.

The door was standing open. 'Anyone home?' he called.

Caro came to the door. She was a small, housewifey-looking woman. No one could have guessed by just looking at her that her exquisite pottery sold for large sums, as did her small paintings of birds and flowers.

'Oh, it's you,' she said. 'What do you want?'

'A wee chat.'

Caro suddenly grinned. 'How nice to be in the Highlands where a policeman asks for a wee chat instead of saying severely, *We want you to accompany us down to the station.* Come in.'

Hamish walked into the living-room-cum-kitchen. It was strange, he thought, that Caro could produce her miracles in such a cramped environment, and then realized there wasn't a potter's wheel, easel, paints, or brushes. As if reading his thoughts, Caro said, 'I've got a

* See *Death of a Dreamer.*

big shed out the back now where I work.
Coffee?'

'Yes, that would be grand.'

'It's ready. I was just about to take a cup myself.'

Hamish took off his cap and settled himself at a table by the window. Outside, he could see Lugs and Sonsie playing in the heather.

Caro put down a mug of coffee in front of him and looked out of the window as well. 'Aren't you frightened that one day that cat is going to revert to the wild and savage your dog?'

'No. It's odd, I know, but they're great friends.'

She sat down opposite him. 'So what brings you?'

'Captain Henry Davenport.'

'Oh, him.'

'Yes, him. Did he con any money out of you?'

There was a long silence.

Then she said with a weary note in her voice. 'I may as well tell you. Knowing you of old, I've a nasty feeling if I don't, you'll dig and dig until you get at the truth.'

'What happened?'

'I arrived back here shortly before he was murdered. It was one of those rare warm days with a breeze blowing all the way in from the Gulf Stream. I like walking. I love the clean air up here. I also wanted to work off my fury. A gallery in Mayfair had promised to hold an exhibition of my paintings. They cancelled at the last minute. They wanted instead to use my space for an exhibition by a sort of Turner Prize artist – you know the type of thing, a painting made from elephant dung and an unmade bed. It was like a slap in the face. They said my little paintings were too "pretty-pretty" for their clients. I was up in the hills where you can look down on Drim and that sinister sea loch when I saw this tweedy sort of military man approaching.

'He stopped and said, "You've been crying. What's the matter?" And he had an English accent.'

'Did that make a difference? We don't go in for English-bashing up here.'

'I know. But you Highlanders run on a different wavelength. It's my own fault. I'm a solitary person. I like my own company. But I suddenly desperately needed someone to talk to. He had a soothing voice. He said he had recently moved to Drim and wondered if he had made a mistake. He said the locals were a bit weird and he always felt he was somehow on the outside looking in. I began to tell him about the gallery rejecting my work. He was so sympathetic that a lot of the pain began to ease. Then to my amazement, he said he knew the owner of the Collin Gallery in Mayfair and he could get me an exhibition but it would take a bit of bribery. He winked at me and I began to laugh. I was feeling so relieved at being able to unburden myself.

'"How much?" I asked.

'"If I could slip him a couple of thousand cash, the deed's done," he said. He introduced himself and handed me his card. It said CAPTAIN HENRY DAVENPORT, FINANCIAL ADVISOR, and gave an address in Guildford. He said he still had a house down there and Drim was really just a holiday home. Now, I keep a few thousand here, or rather I did, for expenses. Everyone wants to be paid off the books these days. Also, I earn an awful lot of money from my pottery so two thousand doesn't mean much to me. I took him back to the house.'

'Oh, dearie, dearie me,' said Hamish. 'Where did you keep it?'

She pointed to a row of white and blue enamel tins on the dresser. 'In the one marked FLOUR. So I got out the money and paid him. He took a note of my phone number and said he'd be in touch but to give him a week.

'Now, when I was out of his orbit, so to speak, I couldn't believe I had been so silly as to trust a complete stranger like that but I decided to give it a chance. About five days later, I went to take out some money and go shopping down in Inverness for some more art supplies. I found all the money in the flour tin was gone.'

'How much?'

'About five thousand.'

120

'Was the door forced?'

'No, but I didn't used to lock it. I do now. I was sure it couldn't have been one of the workmen. How mad! I was always so careful with *them*, the innocents! I would never let them know there was money in the house. I would always say, "Come back tomorrow after I've been to the bank and I'll pay you." So I headed for Drim.'

'I suppose he denied the whole thing.'

'He couldn't. I walked over and when I reached the rise above Drim and looked down, I could see police cars, police tape, and flashing lights. I thought, he's been caught out at last. I didn't want to tell you. People who've been tricked like me feel such fools. Then on the evening news on television, I heard about his murder. I suppose now you'll want to take me in.'

Hamish surveyed her small figure. 'If I thought for a moment you would have the strength to stuff a man of the captain's size up his own chimney, I'd take you down to police headquarters for questioning. We'll keep this quiet for the moment. Milly Davenport is trying to repay money to other victims, but she's not that well off and you can afford it so I won't be telling her, either.'

'Thank you. I can't believe I let myself get tricked by that man. But he seemed capable of exuding a sort of warmth and comfort and I did need a shoulder to cry on.'

'It's the cruelty of it!' exclaimed Hamish. 'A wee bit here, a wee bit there, like a magpie. You'd think he'd use his nasty talents to go for the big time. Oh, he duped his Army friends all right, but I would have thought he would be the sort to go in for some really massive scam.'

'Maybe he did,' said Caro. 'Maybe one of the four men I heard about actually parted with a great deal more than he's saying.'

'It's a thought.'

The corpse of Betty Close lay undisturbed on the bottom of the Gareloch until the canvas of the cheap suitcase she had been packed in finally gave way. The material of the case was already rotted from the salt water, and the pressure from the gases of the decomposing body inside finally burst it open. The corpse floated up to the surface and was borne on a gentle current to a pebbly beach, where it was discovered by a woman walking her dog.

The police were quickly called. The body was naked, and there was not one single sign of identification.

Elspeth, reading out the news that evening, felt a frisson of shock. For some reason, her thoughts flew to Hamish telling her about the murder of the prostitute. Betty Close had not come back to work. It was generally assumed that she had gone off somewhere in a huff.

When she had finished reading the news, Elspeth went back to her dressing room after getting a note of Betty's home address and phoned a police inspector she knew. She told him it was a long shot but that they had a missing researcher called Betty Close and gave him the address.

Then she phoned Hamish Macbeth.

Chapter Seven

Down to Gehenna or up to the Throne,
He travels the fastest who travels alone.
— RUDYARD KIPLING

It was a slow process before the body was finally identified as that of Betty Close.

Jimmy Anderson called round one evening to give Hamish the news.

'I chust knew it!' cried Hamish. 'I guessed she must ha' been listening in when I was telling Elspeth about the idea I had that the death of yon prostitute was somehow linked to the murders.'

'We're not going to get anywhere with that, Hamish.'

'Why?'

'Blair is jumping on the idea. "What proof?" he asks Daviot. "Jist some intuition of some Highland loon." Daviot is anxious not to tread on the toes of another police force. Strathclyde police are investigating, he says, and they are very efficient and that's the end of that.'

'I swear to God,' said Hamish passionately, 'that one of those four men is involved, if not all.'

'Hamish, calm down. Ever since that business with your friend Angela, you've been turning your mind away from the locals.'

'Maybe,' said Hamish with sudden mildness. 'Could be.'

After Jimmy had left, Hamish phoned Angela. 'I'm thinking of taking a wee trip tomorrow,' he began. But Angela interrupted crossly, saying, 'No, I cannot keep an eye on your beasties. I am due in Edinburgh tomorrow. More discussion on the launch of the book.'

'Now, there's an odd thing,' said Hamish. 'I was just thinking of a trip to Edinburgh myself. Could you give me a lift?'

'Yes, I'd be glad of the company. I'll be leaving at eight in the morning.'

'That's grand. I'll be outside your house then. We can share the driving.'

Hamish then phoned Willie Lamont at the Italian restaurant and asked if he would periodically check on the dog and cat the following day.

'I'll do that,' said Willie.

'And I'll leave food for them, so don't be feeding them. Lugs is getting a bit fat.'

'Aye, they're a rare pair of goormitts.'

'Gourmets.'

'Whateffer.'

* * *

126

It was a lovely morning when Hamish walked along the waterfront to Angela's home. A delicate mist was rising from the loch, where the calm waters were broken by a couple of seals.

He wished with all his heart that the murders could be solved and leave him free to return to his old ways of lazing around and enjoying the scenery.

Angela was already sitting in her car. 'New car?' asked Hamish, getting in the front seat of the Ford Escort.

'New second-hand,' said Angela, moving off.

The Currie sisters watched them go from behind their lace curtains. 'You don't think . . . ?' asked Jessie.

'I wouldn't put anything past thon policeman,' said Nessie. 'He's a philanderer.' They decided to go along to Patel's shop and spread a bit of speculative gossip.

Angela's publisher was fortuitously situated in the Royal Mile. Because the famous street was a pedestrian area, Angela found a car park near the Cowgate and they walked together up the High Street, as the Royal Mile was also called. Angela's publisher had offices in the Grassmarket. Hamish agreed to meet her at four in the afternoon. Angela had said she would be having a working lunch in her publisher's offices. Hamish, as he headed for the Canongate, realized he was very hungry. He found a small trendy café that, unfortunately for his rather debased food tastes, turned out to be vegetarian. He reminded himself severely that it was time he switched to eating healthy food and ordered vegetable soup followed by cauliflower and cheese.

Then he left the café and found the address where the prostitute had been murdered.

He walked into the close and then up to the tenement. Like Betty, he found that everyone seemed to be out except for a man who lived under the prostitute's flat.

Hamish produced his warrant card and then asked politely, 'May I come in?'

It was the same balding, black-eyed man that Betty had seen. But Hamish did not know that.

'No,' he said curtly. 'I'm busy.'

Hamish raised his voice to a near shout. 'I am investigating the murder of Betty Close.'

The man grabbed his arm and practically pulled him into the flat. 'All right, all right,' he said.

Hamish walked past him into a narrow corridor. He shut the door. 'In here,' he said. He opened a door into a living room. It was a strangely sterile room: black three-piece leather suite, low glass coffee table, one huge flat-screen TV and stereo system, but no books or pictures.

'What is your name?' asked Hamish.

'John Dean. Why aren't you in uniform?'

'I am Police Sergeant Hamish Macbeth from Lochdubh. I happened to be visiting Edinburgh and thought I would make some inquiries. Did you speak to Betty Close?'

'Who's she?'

Hamish's hazel eyes narrowed. 'Man, it's been in all the papers. She was a television researcher.'

'Oh, I mind. The wee lassie that was found in the Gareloch. Shouldn't you be over there?'

'You haven't answered my question. And there was only a head-and-shoulders picture of her published in the newspapers, so how do you know she was wee?'

'It's just an expression.'

'What do you do for a living, Mr Dean?'

'I'm retired.'

'From what?'

'I owned a disco, Dancing Dirty, down in the Grassmarket.'

'You're in your . . . fifties? Bit young to retire if it was your own business.'

He sighed. 'I wish you'd mind yours. I was bought out.'

'Who bought you out?'

'Scots Entertainment Plc.'

'And where will I find them?'

'Enough!' he shouted. 'Either arrest me and charge me with something or get the hell out of here.'

'You are behaving very suspiciously.'

'Get out!'

* * *

129

Hamish left the flats, went into the nearest shop, and asked if he could look at an Edinburgh telephone directory. Scots Entertainment had offices in Leith Walk. He set off in that direction.

He finally located it with some difficulty because the offices were not actually in Leith Walk itself but in a tenement in a side street. There was a brass plaque on the wall with the name of the company. Hamish walked up the old stone stairs and located the offices on the second floor. He pushed open the door, went in, and blinked at the vision sitting behind the reception desk.

The receptionist was an exquisite blonde wearing a simple black dress and pearls. She had blue eyes in a smooth unlined face. She opened her mouth, which was delicately painted pink, and said, 'Yeah, whit dae ye want?' in a guttural Glaswegian accent.

'I am Police Sergeant Hamish Macbeth. May I be having a wee word wi' your boss?'

'Naw. He's on holiday in the Maldives.'

'And who is standing in for him?'

'Naebody, copper. Push off.'

'You sound as if you've had experience with the police,' said Hamish, 'otherwise you wouldn't be so damn rude.'

'I'm no' paid to be nice. Take a hike.'

Hamish went to a café across Leith Walk where he could sit at the window and get a clear view of the entrance to the offices. The day wore on but no one appeared. Finally, he glanced at his watch and realized that if he did not hurry he would be late to meet Angela. He would need to return home and see if he could get Jimmy interested enough to investigate the background of Scots Entertainment.

As he started walking towards the Royal Mile, he had an uncanny feeling that he was being followed. He whipped around several times but could see no one sinister. He speeded up until he was running fast, threading his way agilely through the crowd. He dived into a doorway, fished out a small camera, and waited. Eventually, he saw a burly man hurrying past. Hamish ran after him, past him, swung around and took a photograph of him, and then ran on. The man pounded after him but was no match for Hamish's speed, for Hamish had won many prizes as a hill runner. He lost the man in the closes off the Mile and then circled back to the parking place where Angela was already waiting for him.

'You're all sweaty, Hamish,' said Angela.

'I was running late,' said Hamish, settling himself into the passenger seat. 'I wish you'd get a bigger car, Angela. My knees are up to my chin.'

'Then get your own car.'

'How did you get on?'

As they drove off, Angela talked excitedly about her working lunch. Hamish only half listened. He would get that photograph developed and see if anything like him turned up in the mug shots in Strathbane.

Late that evening, Hamish sat in a pub in Strathbane, showed Jimmy the photograph he had printed off his digital camera at Patel's, and told him about his day.

'And how am I going to explain your unauthorized visit to Edinburgh?' complained Jimmy.

'Anonymous letter?'

'Saying what exactly?'

'That Scots Entertainment is a front for prostitution.'

'And is it?'

'I have a hunch . . .'

'Oh, spare me your Highland hunches,' groaned Jimmy. 'All right, I'll try it. When can you let me have it?'

'Now,' said Hamish. 'I typed this on one of the old typewriters at the school. I want leave, Jimmy, and urgently. Could you say my aunt in Dornoch is ill?'

'Have you an aunt in Dornoch?'

'She died last year so that makes her as ill as you can get.'

'You're going to Guildford,' said Jimmy accusingly.

'Well, chust let's say, you don't know that.'

Hamish took the long road to Guildford in Surrey early the next morning, after pleading with Willie Lamont again to look after his pets. He flew from Inverness to Gatwick, hired a car with a fleeting thought for his dwindling bank balance, checked his maps, and set out for Guildford. The four men lived in a builder's estate called Surrey Loan on the outskirts of the town. The houses looked expensive but sterile and devoid of character, for despite their size they were all remarkably alike.

The men would not tell him anything, but perhaps they were still out at work and their wives would say something.

He drew a blank at Ferdinand Castle's home. No one was at home. Elspeth had told him that the wives had refused to speak to her. Two streets away, Mrs Bromley, thin and acidic, slammed the door in his face. Through the window, he saw her dialling a number on the telephone. He got the same treatment from Mrs Sanders.

Wearily, he trudged on to the home of Charles Prosser. No one replied. He was just about to turn away when a woman in a four-wheel drive pulled into the short drive.

She got out, exposing a long length of leg.

'Mrs Prosser?' asked Hamish.

Her eyes behind blue contact lenses surveyed the tall policeman with the flaming red hair.

'That's me,' she said huskily.

'I am Police Sergeant Hamish Macbeth and I wanted to ask you a few questions.'

In her high heels, she was almost as tall as Hamish. Everything that could be done to maintain a woman's appearance, from cosmetic surgery to dyed hair, had been achieved and had produced a glamorous effect.

'I say, how exciting. Are you going to put me in handcuffs?'

'Not I,' said Hamish.

Her collagen-plumped lips expanded in a smile. 'Pity. Come inside and we'll have a drink or something.'

In the hall, she shrugged off her coat. She was wearing a low-necked blouse in a leopard-skin print with very tight jeans. She bent over in front of Hamish to slip off her high-heeled shoes, revealing two very round, very firm breasts. Silicone, thought Hamish cynically. He remembered from the notes he had read that her name was Sandra and that she was fifty-two years old.

'Come through to the kitchen,' she said, leading the way.

The kitchen was large and square and full of every labour-saving device.

'Coffee, or something stronger?'

'Coffee would be grand.'

The phone rang shrilly. 'Probably some bore,' said Sandra. 'Ignore it.'

Probably Mrs Bromley, thought Hamish.

When the coffee was served, they sat at the kitchen table. 'Now,' said Sandra, 'why are you here?'

'I was visiting an aunt in Guildford and thought I'd check up on a few points. You've been asked this before, but on the night of the murder of Charles Davenport, Mrs Bromley and her husband, Mrs Castle and her husband, John Sanders and Mrs Sanders, and you and your husband Charles were all having dinner together. Here?'

'Well, we met here for drinks and then we all went on to a restaurant.'

'It doesn't say anything about that,' lied Hamish, hoping to dig out information. He took out a sheaf of notes and scanned them.

'Well, we did.'

'What is the name of the restaurant?'

'Timothy's. It's near the town hall.'

'So lots of people would have seen you there?'

'Timothy himself can vouch for us.'

'What time was this?'

'About seven in the evening.'

Not time for any of them to get up to the Highlands and back. He realized one of her stockinged feet was caressing his ankle.

Should he? In the line of duty? An image of his former love Priscilla Halburton-Smythe, cool as a mountain stream, rose before his eyes.

He stood up abruptly.

'Thank you for your time, Mrs Prosser.'

'Is that all? Don't you want to stay, copper?'

'People to meet, things to do,' gabbled Hamish, heading rapidly for the front door.

He had no sooner gone than the phone began to ring again. It was Mrs Bromley. 'There's some Highland copper snooping around,' she said.

'Yes,' said Sandra. 'I know.'

'You didn't speak to him, did you?'

Sandra hesitated only a moment. 'No, of course not.'

Hamish found Timothy's restaurant and asked to speak to the owner. Timothy was squat and balding. He had a heavy accent. Hamish decided he might be Greek or Turkish. To Hamish's questions he replied testily that he had already gone over everything with the police. So Sandra had lied. Why? The police knew about the restaurant.

What a wasted trip, thought Hamish. He had walked a few steps away from the restaurant when a thin, sallow-faced young man with thick oily hair grabbed his arm. 'I want to sell you a bit of info,' he whispered.

Now, thought Hamish, a proper copper would tell him it was his duty to report what he knew and drag him off to the Guildford police. On the other hand, he was not supposed to be in Guildford.

They walked along the street. 'How much?' asked Hamish.

'A hundred.'

'Fifty or nothing,' said Hamish, noticing that the pupils of the man's eyes were like pinpoints.

'All right. Give it to me.'

'There's a café ower there,' said Hamish. 'Let's sit down. Information first. And if it's not worth anything, nothing is what you're going to get.'

The café was of the kind with a bewildering array of expensively priced coffee. Hamish ordered an Americana and his companion, a cappuccino.

'What have you got?' asked Hamish. 'First of all, your name?'

'Stefan Loncar.'

'So what information do you have for me?'

'That bastard, Timothy, sacked me last week. Says if I talk to the police, he'll cut my balls off. But I'm going back to Zagreb tomorrow. I need money.'

'So what have you got?'

'Those four men and their wives, the ones the police were asking about, they dined that evening in a private room upstairs.'

Hamish felt a flicker of excitement.

'Were they all there?'

'There were the four of them. I recognized the wives. But the men were all wearing funny masks.'

'What! Why?'

'They were laughing and said they'd just come from a fancy dress party.'

'But people who dined in the restaurant on the same night couldn't remember seeing them. Surely they would remember four men in masks.'

'There's a back stair leading from the car park that goes up to the private room. The police were happy to take Timothy's word for it. Thomas Bromley paid for the dinner with his credit card. Timothy showed that to the police as proof but he said nothing about the private room. Where's my money?'

'Aren't you worried? One of them could be a murderer.'

'I'm off to Zagreb in the morning.'

Hamish took out a battered wallet and extracted two twenty-pound notes and a ten. Stefan snatched them and ran out of the café. Hamish hurried after him but when he got outside, Stefan seemed to have disappeared into thin air.

* * *

The four wives got together for drinks that afternoon. 'Did you tell your husbands?' asked Sandra.

'Not yet,' said Mary Bromley.

'Don't let's,' said Sandra. 'It's not safe. I think we should all keep quiet.'

Reluctantly, the others agreed.

Hamish Macbeth walked round to the back of the restaurant and studied the staircase. There was no CCTV camera. There was now possibly a fifth man involved, one who perhaps took the place of whoever it was that had gone to Scotland to murder Captain Davenport.

He experienced a feeling of relief. One of the four must have committed the murder, which left the locals clear of suspicion. Now he had to head north and try to pass on what he had learned without betraying that he had strayed out of his area.

As soon as he got back to Lochdubh, he called Jimmy and told him to come to the police station in the morning. He locked up his sleepy hens, refused to feed Lugs, who was getting fat, even though the dog banged his feeding bowl on the floor, then he showered and went to bed. But he did not fall asleep immediately. If Sandra Prosser told her husband of his visit, then Charles Prosser might complain to the Guildford police, and then one Highland police sergeant would be in trouble. But if one of the men was a murderer and the others were hiding the fact and colluding with him, then Hamish doubted the Guildford police would learn anything. What about those masks, though? Britain had more spy cameras on its streets than any other country. Surely the men had been questioned about the masks.

Jimmy arrived at ten in the morning, his blue eyes bloodshot and his clothes looking as if they had been slept in.

'Hard night?' asked Hamish.

'Don't want to talk about it,' mumbled Jimmy. 'What's up?'

Hamish described what he had found in Guildford. Jimmy groaned and clutched his head. 'What am I to do with all this?' he demanded. 'Poaching on Guildford's territory.'

'Never mind. I've got a nice anonymous letter all written out for you. I want you to phone Guildford and the police at Gatwick airport and stop Stefan Loncar from getting on that plane.'

'He may already have gone.'

'I checked. It's due to leave at noon today.'

'Right. Give me the letter. I hope there's no fingerprints and no DNA.'

'Of course not. Your name's been mentioned in the press so I put it on the envelope. Off you go. Oh, there's one thing. Why weren't the police suspicious about those masks the men were wearing?'

'It never came up. The camera focused on the front of the restaurant wasn't working. And if, as you say, they went up a back stair, it doesn't matter anyway.'

When he had gone, Hamish switched on his computer and studied the little information he had about the four men. Thomas Bromley ran a chain of clothing stores. But did he have other businesses? Was Timothy's one of his? If that was the case, it would explain why Timothy was prepared to lie for him. Timothy had claimed in a statement to Guildford police that he was the owner. Hamish googled a list of Guildford restaurants, and his hazel eyes gleamed. Timothy's was not listed, and yet he had a feeling in his bones that it was owned or part owned by one of the men. He needed a business expert to search company directories and find what other companies might belong to the men and if they had any connection with Scotland.

Prosser's supermarkets were called Foodies but all of them were in the south of England. There was no connection, then, with Scotland.

Hamish had a feeling that the captain had actually got much more money out of one or all of them for some scam, more money than they claimed to have lost. The lawyers' letters from the four had all been dated last year.

Maybe the captain had come up with a get-rich-quick scheme for them. Persuading them that it was so good that they could not only recoup their losses but gain a fortune. From people like Angela and Edie and Caro, he had gathered that the captain had been superb as a con artist.

He went out for a walk and met Angela Brodie on the waterfront. Her thin face was alight with excitement. 'Hamish, my publisher thinks my book might be nominated for the Haggart Prize.'

'That's grand, Angela. What's it about?'

'Oh, the usual this and that.'

'Like what?'

'Oh, Hamish, literary books are so hard to describe.'

'Try me.'

'Oh, there's Mrs Wellington. I must ask her about something.'

Hamish studied her retreating figure suspiciously. He suddenly felt sure that Angela's novel was based on Lochdubh, maybe a thinly disguised Lochdubh. He was in the clear because writers only brought policemen into detective stories, and detective writers never got literary awards.

He rubbed his face and neck with midge repellent because the day was soft and damp and those Scottish mosquitoes were out in force. A thin line of mist lay across the forest on the opposite bank. Two seals struggled on to a rock by the beach and stared at him with big round eyes. He turned away. A little part of his brain was superstitious and believed the old stories that the seals were dead people who had come back.

He collected his dog and cat and drove to Drim. He let them out on the beach to play and went to Milly's house.

Hamish frowned when he recognized Tam's car parked outside. He didn't quite trust Tam or, for that matter, any other reporter except Elspeth. He wanted to phone Elspeth and ask her if she knew any business experts but – remembering the fate of Betty Close – decided he might be putting her in danger.

Milly answered the door. Her face was flushed and her eyes bright. 'Come in, Hamish. You'll find Tam in the kitchen.'

'I would like a word with you in private. Did your husband leave any business papers? Did the police take them away?'

'Apart from bank statements and bills and things like that, there wasn't much else.'

Tam appeared in the doorway. Hamish had a sudden idea. 'Tam, do you know anyone expert enough to dig into company registers and find maybe hidden companies?'

'Why?'

'I can't be telling you the noo but if you help me, you'll be the first to get the news if anything breaks.'

Tam scratched one of his large ears. 'I mind there's a retired businessman up at Craskie in a wee white cottage called Cruachan, just on the left as you approach the village. He's called John McFee.'

'Thanks. I'll try him.'

Hamish drove off and took the coast road to Craskie. He spotted the cottage easily. An elderly gentleman with white hair was working in his front garden.

'Mr McFee,' called Hamish.

'Aye, that's me.'

He straightened up from weeding, groaned, and clutched his back. 'Age is a terrible thing, laddie. How can I help you? I can't be frightened at the sight of a policeman because there's simply no one left in my life I care about.'

Will I be like this some day? wondered Hamish. *Will there be anyone in my life to care for me?*

He stood with one foot raised and his mouth slightly open.

'Don't stand there looking glaikit,' said John. 'Come ben the house. The midges out here are eating me alive.'

Hamish followed him into a book-lined living room. There was a peat fire on the hearth and several good pieces of furniture. 'Sit at the table at the window,' ordered John, 'and I'll get us some coffee. I don't like these coffee tables. Can't stand bending over to drink coffee. Listen to that. The wind's rising. I hope it blows those damn midges out to sea. Do midges have a natural predator?'

'I don't know,' said Hamish. 'I've never really thought about it.'

'I'll get the coffee.'

Hamish took off his hat and put it on the floor at his feet. The cottage was on a slight rise and afforded a good view of the sea. A patch of blue sky was forming to the west, and seagulls wheeled and dived over the rising waves.

His eyes began to droop and he fell suddenly asleep, waking only when John put a tray of coffee and biscuits on the table.

'Sorry,' said Hamish. 'A bad night.'

'So what brings you?' asked John, pouring coffee. There was no evidence of central heating, and the fire gave out little heat. He was wearing two sweaters and thick trousers.

'I need your expertise,' said Hamish. 'You'll have heard about the murders.'

'Yes, bad business.'

'I want to tell you what I know about four men and then hope you can somehow find out which companies they own, particularly if one of them has an umbrella company that covers the fact that he owns a restaurant in Guildford called Timothy's.'

'Won't your headquarters have experts?'

'Not that I know of. There's another thing. The four men sent lawyers' letters to the

145

captain, but the demands for repayment did not involve a great deal of money. To have killed Captain Davenport in such a vicious rage leads me to believe that he scammed a great deal of money for some venture out of all of them. If you agree, I will arrange some form of payment for you from Strathbane.'

John sighed. 'I'm so bored these days, I would do it for nothing.'

'I want you to be very careful,' warned Hamish. 'Don't get close to any of these men or their business. One of them, I am sure, is a murderer.'

Back at the police station, Hamish waited and waited to hear from Jimmy. 'I'm coming right over,' said the detective. 'Blair's furious. He wanted it to be one of the villagers. He says the letter is just mad spite but Daviot has sent it off to Guildford. See you soon.'

Jimmy arrived just as the wind had risen to a full gale. 'How you can live here beats me,' he complained. 'Why is it so cold? It's summer.'

'Global cooling,' said Hamish. 'What have you got?'

'First of all, something bad. Stefan Loncar was booked on the noon plane to Zagreb but didn't turn up. They searched his flat. He had packed up but there was no sign of him.'

'Someone must have spied me talking to him,' said Hamish.

'Maybe. The four suspects have been brought in for questioning. They lawyered up immediately. It's English law, see? They don't need to wait until we allow them lawyers.'

'What about the masks? And what fancy dress party were they coming from?'

'They now say there wasn't any party. They'd been watching the Iraq inquiry and they had these Tony Blair masks and thought it would be a bit of a hoot to wear them. They are all members of the Rotary Club and the Freemasons and you name it. Guildford said they had to let them go.'

Hamish told him about his visit to John McFee.

'Now, there's a thing,' said Jimmy. 'I wanted to hire an expert but Blair blocked it. Says we haven't the funds.'

'Well, if McFee comes up with anything, you'd better get your chequebook out,' said Hamish. 'I not only want to find out how much Davenport tricked them out of, I want to know if they have any connection to Scotland, Edinburgh in particular. Oh, and did they question Timothy again?'

'Yes, he swears blind the four men are regular customers and salt of the earth. His real name is Andreas Gristedes. Greek by birth. How soon can your expert come up with anything?'

Hamish groaned. 'Probably a month or so. It isn't the telly where some geek flicks through

a computer and says, "Aha!" Why haven't you
asked for whisky?'

'Drying out.'

'About time.'

'So we have to wait.'

Chapter Eight

In married life three is company and two none.
— OSCAR WILDE

Hamish called on John McFee the next day, anxious for some sort of a result.

'It's difficult,' said John. 'I'll let you know when I've got something. You see, you can hide names of any partners. It depends on what kinds of partners you have. For example, you can have active partner, ostensible partner, silent partner, secret partner, dominant partner, and limited partner. You can also pay to have the names of the partners in the company hidden.

'Then if it's that secretive, say for hiding companies or laundering money, you could set everything up in Greek Cyprus or Ukraine. I'll let you know as soon as I get anything.'

When he left John, Hamish stopped on the road back to Lochdubh and called Jimmy. 'My expert's proving slow,' he complained. 'Surely you've got your own man on it.'

149

'Fact is, the whole business has gone on the back burner,' said Jimmy. 'We've got illegal cigarette smugglers and drug smugglers and God knows what other mayhem. The press have forgotten about your case, so the pressure's off.'

When he had rung off, Hamish sat scowling. He got down from the Land Rover and let the dog and cat out. 'Go and play on the beach,' he said. He phoned Elspeth in Glasgow.

'I'm in my dressing room,' said Elspeth. 'I've only got a few minutes.'

'It's like this,' said Hamish. 'Strathbane have dropped investigating the captain's death because the press pressure is off. Can you get it on again?'

'I'll try. Got to go.'

When Hamish returned to Lochdubh, it was to find Angela Brodie pacing up and down outside the police station.

'What's up?' he asked. 'No, you pair,' he shouted at the dog and cat. 'You are *not* going to the Italian restaurant. Get inside. Sorry, Angela. But they're getting ower fat.'

'My husband's got the norovirus.'

'That's bad. But he'll be over it in three days.'

'It's not that. The Haggart dinner is tonight in Edinburgh.'

'And?'

'I don't want to go alone,' said Angela feverishly. 'Would you come with me?'

'I think I could manage that. You're in a right state, Angela. It's not the Booker Prize. The Haggart people sell cakes.'

'Hamish!' said Angela impatiently. 'It's one of the oldest literary awards. Haggart may manufacture cakes but they set up this award in Edwardian days and it's been on the go ever since. I'm tired of being just a nominee. The first book was nominated for the Booker. The one before last for the Haggart. I've got to win.'

'Angela, you never struck me as being ambitious!'

'Now you know.'

'Calm down. I'll go.'

'Oh, thanks. Mrs Wellington is going to check on my husband. We have to be at the Caledonian Hotel for the dinner. It starts at seven o'clock. Can we leave in an hour, say?'

'Won't we be a bit early?'

'It's better to be early. I mean there could be sheep on the road, or a tractor, or fog.'

Hamish looked up at the clear blue sky and then back down at Angela's worried face.

'I'll be ready,' he said gently.

Angela drove most of the way in silence, her knuckles white with tension on the steering wheel. The last time Hamish had seen her in such a state was when she was determined to

be the perfect wife because of the malign influ-
ence of an incomer to the village. But ever
since she had got over that, she had been her
old self, gentle and unassuming and the worst
cook in Sutherland.

She was wearing a pretty, floaty sort of
chiffon dress under her coat along with very
thick make-up. Hamish was wearing a Savile
Row suit that he had picked up in a thrift
shop. The last time he had worn it was the last
time he had met Priscilla for dinner. He had a
sudden sharp longing to speak to her again.

As he had expected, they were too early by
an hour so they went into the hotel bar. 'Better
keep to mineral water,' cautioned Angela,
'because there'll be drinks at dinner and I want
all my wits about me.' She took a sheaf of
notes out of her handbag and began to study
them, her lips moving.

'What's that?' asked Hamish.

'It's my acceptance speech.'

'Angela! You're taking all this too seriously.'

'What would you know? You haven't a
single ambitious bone in your body.'

'Aye, and I like it that way.' Hamish suddenly wished the evening would be over.

At last, they went in for dinner. Angela and
Hamish were seated at one of the round tables
with her publisher, Henry Satherwaite, a thin
female poet called Jemima Thirsk and her
husband, and two Haggart executives and
their wives.

The dinner was at last over and the chairman of Haggart took the podium. He droned on about the virtue of the firm's cakes and then got down to the business of the evening.

'We have five nominees: Jemima Thirsk for her poems, *It Happened One Sunday*, Simon Swallow for *The Bastard of Bridgetown*, Angela Brodie for *The Bovary Factor*, Sean Belfast for *The End of Ulster*, and Harriet Wilson for *Tales from My Cherokee Grandmother*.

'Our distinguished panel of experts have chosen the prizewinner.' With maddening slowness he opened an envelope. 'Get on with it!' muttered Angela, polishing off her after-dinner brandy in one gulp.

'The winner is – Harriet Wilson for *Tales from My Cherokee Grandmother*.'

Angela turned chalk-white. Her publisher patted her hand. 'Better luck next year,' he whispered.

Harriet Wilson was a large woman wearing a beaded gown and with two feathers stuck in her elaborately dressed coils of grey hair. She fell over getting up to the platform, and it took two men to hoist her to her feet.

She blinked myopically at the audience and then vomited violently.

'They're always drunks,' said Hamish.

'Why do you say that?' asked Henry.

'Because it's always a Cherokee grandmother. Never the Sioux or the Mohawk or the Cree. Very fertile lady that grandmother.'

'You mean, she might have made the whole thing up?'

'Maybe,' said Hamish. 'Oh, Angela, don't take on so.' For Angela was crying quietly. He put an arm round her and gave her a hug.

'Did you see that?' hissed Nessie Currie, gazing avidly at the television set. 'I knew it. That Hamish Macbeth should be locked up. No woman is safe from him. And there's poor Dr Brodie at death's door. Shame!'

'Shame,' echoed Jessie.

'No wonder herself is crying. It's the shame o' adultery.'

'Adultery,' murmured Jessie.

Dr Brodie was lying on the sofa, feeling like death. His ancient television had broken down right before the screening of the Haggart awards. He heard knocking at the kitchen door but felt too ill to get up so he shouted weakly, 'Come in. It isn't locked.'

And in came some of the villagers bearing cakes and whisky and flowers and home remedies, which they put down on the kitchen table. Mrs Wellington, who had been banished from her duties as doctor-sitter, nonetheless came in and looked sympathetically at Dr Brodie.

'Did she win?' he whispered.

'I'm afraid not.'

'What's everyone doing in the kitchen?'

'Folk are bringing you some things to make you feel better. Have you . . . er . . . read your wife's book?'

'Not yet. Angela doesn't like me reading her stuff until it's published. That's an idea. There's a copy over there. Hand it to me.'

'Well, now, I think you should rest your eyes. I'll just switch on the telly.'

'It's broken down.'

'You need to be firm with these machines.' Mrs Wellington brought her fist down on the top of the machine, and it flickered into life. 'There! That'll soothe you.' She handed him the remote control.

Mrs Wellington tiptoed out. Dr Brodie looked at a programme where two men were beheading a third. He switched it off. He was feeling marginally better. Maybe now was the time to read his wife's book.

Angela rallied for the book signing. To Hamish's relief, she seemed to be signing quite a lot of books. He bought one himself and retreated to a quiet corner. As he read, his eyebrows practically vanished up into his thick, flaming red hair. He skimmed through the book rapidly. It was the story of a bored doctor's wife in a Highland village who embarks on a steamy affair with the village policeman.

The sex scenes were graphic. Either Angela had a vivid imagination or Dr Brodie was more of a stud than anyone could have guessed. He blushed all over. Angela's ambition had made her blind to the effect her book would have on Lochdubh. Hamish could imagine the gossip spreading across the whole of Sutherland.

Henry Satherwaite came up to him. 'Good book, eh? Are you from Lochdubh?'

'I am.'

'What do you do there?'

'I'm the village policeman.'

Henry grinned.

'No, I am not Angela's lover, and this book is going to cause me one shedload of trouble,' said Hamish. 'I . . .' He suddenly saw a familiar face. Simon Swallow, the author, was signing books, and sitting beside him, opening books for him to sign, was the receptionist from Scots Entertainment. She saw him and got to her feet. Hamish tried to catch her but she vanished into the ladies' toilet. He waited outside, then opened the door and went in. Two women at the hand basins let out a screech of protest. Hamish flashed his warrant card before checking the cubicles. Then he noticed a blast of cold air. The room was L-shaped. He turned the corner. A window was standing open. He leaned out. There was a fire escape to the car park. As he watched, a black BMW went roaring off.

He returned to the signing and picked up a copy of Simon Swallow's book. There was now only one woman in front of him. When it was his turn, Simon asked, 'Who's it to?'

Hamish showed his warrant card. 'Who was that girl who was opening the books for you?'

'Oh, Sonia. Where's she gone and what do you want with her?'

'Just a wee chat.'

'She's probably gone to the toilet.'

'Sonia took one look at me and ran off and escaped out the toilet window. How do you know her?'

'We met up in a pub this lunchtime and she offered tae come along.'

Hamish retreated to a corner of the room and phoned John McFee. 'Concentrate on a firm called Scots Entertainment,' he said. 'There's something fishy about it.'

'Will do.'

'And get back to me as soon as possible.'

He waited until Angela had signed her last book. 'They've booked rooms here for us for the night,' said Angela, 'but I must get home.'

'All right. But I'll drive.'

In the car, as he drove off out of Edinburgh and took the long road north, Hamish said, 'Angela, I don't want to add to your distress, but have you any idea what's waiting for us in Lochdubh? You wrote about a doctor's wife having an affair with a policeman. You're going to be damned as the whore of Lochdubh.'

'But they all know me!' wailed Angela. 'They cannot possibly think—'

'Oh, yes they can. Oh, dinnae greet. You must have cried a bucketful already,' said Hamish heartlessly.

Angela snivelled, blew her nose, and said, 'I must have gone mad. What's it like, Hamish, to have no ambition whatsoever?'

'It makes a man enjoy the day. Ambition can cause envy and resentment. Chust look at the mess you're in. Try to get some sleep.'

As Hamish drove up the steep road that wound through the hills towards Lairg, he glanced in dismay at the petrol gauge. He hoped there was just enough fuel to get them home.

Then he saw the lights of a car coming up fast behind them. He had a sudden premonition of disaster before the car struck them and sent them crashing over the side of the road and down a steep brae. Angela's little car hit a rock, somersaulted, and landed on its roof. Cursing, Hamish unfastened his seat belt and managed to get the door open. He heard his attacker roar off into the distance. He rolled out into the heather. He could hardly believe that he hadn't broken anything. He went round to the passenger side and wrenched open the door. He unfastened Angela's seat belt and eased her out. 'What happened?' she asked.

'Have you broken anything?'

'I think I'm all right. I feel so sick.'

'Chust lie down in the heather away from the car. I don't think it's going to burst into flames but you never know.'

He phoned the police emergency number and demanded all the services fast: police, fire, and ambulance.

Then he phoned Jimmy Anderson's mobile number and told a sleepy Jimmy all about the girl at the book signing and the attack on them. 'Get the Edinburgh police to check immediately on Scots Entertainment and find that girl, Sonia,' said Hamish. 'Someone tried to kill us.'

'Saw you on the telly at the awards hugging Angela. You sure it wasn't Dr Brodie?'

'He's in bed sick and why would it be him?'

'There was talk about the book. Seems your pal has written about a Highland policeman rogering the doctor's wife.'

'Drop it, Jimmy. I swear to God it's one of those four bastards. Any sign of Stefan Loncar?'

'Not a one. His permit was about to run out so we think he may have gone into hiding.'

'I think you should be looking for a body,' said Hamish.

Hamish rang off when he heard sirens in the distance. First on the scene was the Lairg volunteer fire brigade. Hamish told them to leave the car where it was, as the Scenes Of Crime Operatives would need to examine the whole place first. He was just about to ask them to take Angela to hospital when two police cars arrived and then a mountain rescue helicopter. Hamish insisted that Angela go to hospital as she was now feeling sick and was plainly in a state of shock. After she had been borne off, he made a full statement to the police and asked to be driven to Lochdubh. The scene was suddenly floodlit as a television team arrived.

Oh, the magic of television, thought Hamish bitterly as some of the police began obviously posing for the camera. He was glad to see the formidable figure of Police Inspector Mary Benson climbing out of the car. She shouted at the television crew to get back up on the road and stop compromising a crime scene or she would have them all arrested.

Hamish had to tell his story all over again. 'And how come you recognized this girl and how did you know she worked for Scots Entertainment?'

Cautiously, Hamish explained that he had been escorting Angela to her publisher and had decided to pass the time by interviewing the neighbours in a close in the Canongate where Betty Close might have been last seen. The one neighbour in the flat under where a prostitute had been murdered had said he worked for Scots Entertainment, so he had gone to have a look at their offices and it was there that he had seen Sonia.

'I can't understand all this and what led you to think that the death of a prostitute in an Edinburgh tenement should have anything to do with the murder of Captain Davenport. Give me a full report tomorrow.'

After she had read the news bulletin the next day, Elspeth went to her dressing room. What on earth was Hamish Macbeth doing? Was he having an affair with Angela? They had always been very close. Surely not. The door of her dressing room opened, and her boss walked in. 'You'd best get up to Lochdubh,' he said. 'You know this copper. Great stuff.'

'It's hardly a great Hollywood-type scandal,' protested Elspeth.

'Come on. Madame Bovary in a wee Highland village? Get going.'

Priscilla Halburton-Smythe, sitting at her computer desk in a London office, got a call from her father. 'Heard the latest about Hamish Macbeth?' he demanded and, without waiting for her reply, gave her a highly embroidered account of the scandal, ending with, 'It was the best thing that ever happened when you broke off your engagement to Macbeth.'

'He broke it off,' protested Priscilla.

'Thank goodness, you're well out of it,' remarked her father.

Hamish was ordered by Daviot to stay locked inside his police station until headquarters drafted out a statement to defuse the scandal. Still shocked after the accident, Hamish stayed in bed, only rousing himself when he heard Jimmy's voice on his answering machine saying he was outside the police-station door.

Hamish let him in and slammed the door in the faces of the press.

'You look like shit,' he said cheerfully, 'but things are moving. Edinburgh police said the offices of Scots Entertainment were closed down. The man you took a photo of has been identified as Nick Duke, a villain who now seems to have disappeared. They raided the offices of Scots Entertainment and found it was a front for a brothel, but no girls were to be found and the safe was empty. That chap John Dean, who lived under where yon prostitute was killed, has vanished as well.'

'Not much farther forward,' said Hamish gloomily.

'It shows you were right. It all ties together. So what the hell have you been up to?'

'Nothing. Angela's a dear friend. I could wring her neck for landing me in this mess.'

'Cheer up. There's good news.'

'I could do with some.'

'Angela Brodie woke up in the Raigmore Hospital in Inverness and who does she find sitting by her bed but Blair.'

'What?'

'He says she should get her revenge on you for leading her astray and wets his fat lips and asks for all the juicy details. Now, Angela's got a wee tape recorder in her handbag and switches it on. She'd been taping the awards ceremony. "Explain yourself," she says.

'He says that everyone now knows that Macbeth has been getting into her knickers, and then his remarks got even cruder and dirtier. So when she thinks she's got enough, she presses the buzzer and orders him out. Then she phones Daviot and plays the tape. Daviot hits the roof and suspends Blair.'

'Where's Angela now?'

'She checked out and she's back home.'

Hamish's answering machine sounded again. Elspeth's voice: 'Hamish, I'm up in the fields at the back. If you open the kitchen window, I can get in that way. I know I can get you out of this.'

'Daviot says you're not to speak to the press,' said Jimmy.

'Oh, she won't do anything I don't want.' Hamish opened the kitchen window.

After five minutes, Elspeth climbed in. She looked more like the Elspeth Hamish once knew rather than the sophisticated television presenter she had become. The day was damp and drizzly, and her hair was once more frizzy. She was wearing an anorak over a sweater and cords.

'So what's the latest?' she asked breathlessly. 'I've just been sent back up here.'

'I have to stay locked in here and not speak to the press,' said Hamish.

'That'll make things worse. I'm supposed to get you, Angela, and Dr Brodie together to make a statement and scotch this scandal. The public have only got to see Angela and her husband together with you to show everyone it's all a load of rubbish.'

'Daviot'll go mad,' said Hamish.

'I'll fix him. I'll just use your office.' She went into the police-station office and slammed the door.

'Whisky?' demanded Jimmy.

'Aye, I could do with a dram.' Hamish lifted down the bottle and put three glasses on the table.

He was just pouring when Elspeth re-appeared looking triumphant. 'It's all fixed.'

'How did you manage it?'

'Daviot is to appear with you. He loves the idea of being on television. He said he would be glad to let the matter be settled. He will give Angela all the help she needs provided she doesn't sue them for Blair's behaviour.'

'So where's the filming to take place?'

'The Tommel Castle Hotel.'

'And how do you get me and the Brodies up there without the other press crowding in?'

'Daviot is sending a police car to take the Brodies to a private room at the hotel. I'll have my crew already in there and set up. The press will follow, but they'll be locked out.'

'Then they'll all write spoiling stories.'

'Daviot's bringing lawyers to have a word with them all afterwards. They'll need to be careful.'

'So how do we get there?'

'Out the window, Hamish. I've got a four-wheel drive parked up in the fields. Also, you wanted press pressure on the police to solve the murders. Here's your chance.'

Elspeth was glad she had brought a make-up artist with her because Angela looked a wreck. Her flyaway hair was even more dishevelled and her face was white and drawn. Dr Brodie had not quite recovered from his attack of the norovirus, and he looked weak and shaky.

Only Daviot looked happy, surrendering to the ministrations of the make-up artist and getting his silver hair brushed till it shone.

'I think you should go first, Angela,' said Elspeth. 'Tell the folks about being a writer and how you used the local colour and your experiences of being a doctor's wife.'

'Must I?' asked Angela in a low voice.

'This scandal has to be stopped,' said

165

Elspeth. 'Oh, I phoned your publisher. Sales of your books are good.'

'They are?'

'Right up there.'

Angela came over well. Heartened by the news of her sales, protective of her husband, she described how the plot had come about. She held her husband's hand throughout.

Daviot then spoke and said that Hamish Macbeth was a valued officer and a model of good behaviour. When he had finished, he added magnanimously, 'Would you like to say a few words, Mr Macbeth?'

Hamish had more than a few words to say. After describing the Brodies as old and valued friends, he then said, 'I would like to make an appeal to the public.'

'Is this about the murders?' asked Elspeth.

'Yes.' Hamish described everything he had found out from the murder of Captain Davenport right up to the attack on him and Angela. He linked the murders of Philomena Davenport, Betty Close, and the prostitute. He appealed for anyone with news about Scots Entertainment to come forward and anyone who also had information about the missing John Dean.

Elspeth wound up the interviews, holding up a copy of Angela's book and urging people to buy it while stocks lasted.

Mr Johnson, the manager, then served sandwiches and drinks. 'I will just make a statement to the press outside,' said Daviot, and he left the room followed by his lawyers.

Lochdubh had watched the whole thing on television with great feelings of disappointment. There was no doubting the sincerity of Hamish or the Brodies. Mutterings about the presents given to Dr Brodie spread around the village. Archie Maclean, the fisherman, was ordered to go to the doctor's and take back the cod he had given him. Timid Archie lied and said it had been eaten.

And Police Sergeant Hamish Macbeth returned wearily to his police station and prayed that something would break so that the shadow of murder could leave. He decided that Strathbane were not going to inflict another policeman on him, as Tolly, his former constable, had taken early retirement. He had already sent Tolly's belongings to him. He dragged out several items of furniture but then realized he was very tired and left them sitting on his living-room floor.

Chapter Nine

And almost every one when age,
Disease, or sorrows strike him,
Inclines to think there is a God,
Or someone very like him.
— ARTHUR HUGH CLOUGH

Impatient for news, the following day Hamish decided to visit John McFee and find out what was taking him so long.

He drove over to Craskie. The day was so sunny and fine that somehow it seemed to intensify his worries. The normally heaving Atlantic, where some of the old people still believed the blue men rode the waves, was docile and temporarily tamed. The mountains of Sutherland soared up majestically to a clear blue sky. Even the normally wheeling, screeching gulls seemed to be silent. It was as if the whole of nature had paused to enjoy the beauty of this rare summer's day.

Hamish knocked at John's door and waited. He was just about to knock again when he heard the sound of shuffling footsteps approaching from the other side. The door creaked open and Hamish bit back an exclamation of dismay. John appeared to have dwindled in size. His thick white hair had gone and he was as bald as a coot.

'What's wrong with ye?' demanded Hamish, his voice sharp with anxiety.

'Lung cancer,' said John. 'Come ben.'

He stood aside. Hamish walked into the small cluttered living room. His eyes ranged over the place. He could not see a computer. John slumped in an armchair by the fireplace.

'How long have you known?' asked Hamish.

'Months,' said John wearily. 'The chemo didn't work. I've come home to die.'

'How long have you got?'

'Weeks, maybe months if I'm lucky.' There was an oxygen tank beside his chair. John fumbled with it and attached tubes to his nose.

'Why didn't you tell me, man? I don't see a computer.'

'Fact is, Hamish, I never learned how to use a computer and my old associates, them that aren't dead, couldn't help me.'

'But the wasted time? You should have said something. Why didn't you?'

'I did try my best. It took my mind off my troubles. I felt important. I told the neighbours I was working for the police.'

'Are you getting home help?'

'Yes, I've got a carer. She's off at the shops, and the doctor calls regularly.'

There was silence. The oxygen machine sent out a rhythmic clicking sound. John lay back in his chair and closed his eyes.

Hamish curbed his temper. He could hardly shout about the wasted time, not when the poor man was dying.

'Never mind,' he said. 'I'll be off.'

John opened his eyes and said faintly, 'Do you think there is a God?'

'Maybe,' said Hamish, but once outside he muttered to himself, 'Not right now, I don't.'

Hamish drove to police headquarters in Strathbane, confident that at least he would not run into Blair as, last heard, the man was still suspended. Jimmy was not around so Hamish went to Jimmy's favourite pub and found the detective sitting at a table in the corner.

'Shouldn't you be working?' snapped Hamish, who was still furious over the time John McFee had wasted.

'I'm on my break,' said Jimmy mildly. 'Sit down and stop looming over me.'

'Any news on Scots Entertainment?'

'It's controlled by a company registered in the Ukraine. That's as far as we've got. How's your expert getting on?'

Hamish told him about John McFee.

'Poor auld sod,' said Jimmy. 'Never mind. Your telly appeal has galvanized the experts and we should get something soon, but thae shell companies are the devil.'

Hamish sat down, removed his cap, and put it on the table. 'I've been thinking, Jimmy.'

'Bad sign. Have a drink.'

'I'm driving. I've been thinking that, say those four men were involved and got cheated out of some really serious money. It must have been some sort of big scam, and I think the clue lies in Edinburgh. Maybe it was something other than that gold mine. Now, I mind there's a businessmen's club there, called the Merlin. I wish I could get in there.'

'Aye, and if one of the famous four is there as well and spots you, you might not get back to Lochdubh in one piece.'

'I could go in disguise. I'm a rare hand at the disguises.'

Jimmy looked cynically at Hamish's flaming red hair. 'I could spot ye a mile off. Forget it, Hamish. Remember the tongue twister? The Leith police dismisseth us? It'll be nothing to what Edinburgh police'll do if you poach on their territory. There's already been rumblings about you snooping around the Canongate and Scots Entertainment without telling them. They learned about that somehow.'

'Just an idea,' said Hamish vaguely. 'Let me know as soon as you get anything.'

* * *

Back at the police station, he phoned David Harrison, who owned a large factory outside Edinburgh that manufactured goods for the tourist trade. David had once been on holiday in Lochdubh, and they had spent some time fishing together.

Hamish explained that he'd like to disguise himself as a wealthy businessman, Scottish but visiting from Canada, to get an entrée to the Merlin Club. 'I could take you along tomorrow for lunch and get you booked in as a temporary member,' said David. 'I'm busy at the moment, but meet me there and tell me all about it tomorrow.'

When he had rung off, Hamish rang Elspeth. 'We're just about to leave,' she said.

'I want the services of your make-up artist,' said Hamish. He rapidly told her his plan.

'That sounds exciting. We'll hang on. I'll tell them it's for amateur theatricals.'

At the hotel, he spoke to the manager first. 'Does Priscilla's uncle, Bartholomew Smythe, still keep some of his stuff here?'

'Aye, it's in a trunk in the basement.'

'Priscilla,' lied Hamish, 'said it would be all right if I borrowed a few things.'

'Go ahead. Here's the key to the cellar. It's the big black steamer trunk in the corner. What are you up to?'

'I'll tell you when it's all over.'

In the cellar, Hamish selected two suits and a tuxedo, two shirts, and two pairs of shoes, grateful that the uncle took the same size in footwear. He left them all in reception, then phoned Elspeth and said he was ready. He finally emerged from the ministrations of the make-up artist with black hair, a thin black moustache, a large pair of spectacles, and pads to pump up his cheeks.

Back at the police station, he phoned Willie at the restaurant and begged him to take care of Sonsie and Lugs on the following day.

The next day, wearing his new disguise, he put on a beautifully cut tweed suit and brogues. The suit looked as if it had been tailored for him. Now for Edinburgh, he thought.

David Harrison stared in amazement at Hamish. 'I wouldn't have recognized you! Now, what's it all about?'

As Hamish told him, his eyes ranged over the other diners. The club was situated in Charlotte Square in the New Town. Expensive men in expensive suits, Rolex watches, well-fed faces, discreet murmur of voices.

'See anyone?' asked David.

'No,' said Hamish, thinking miserably that it had all been a waste of time and effort.

'You keep talking about four men. Why don't you give me their names? I might recognize one of them.'

'John Sanders, Charles Prosser, Thomas Bromley, and Ferdinand Castle.'

'One of those names rings a bell. Stop look-ing so miserable and eat your steak and let me think.'

David was a very small man, just five feet tall, with thick brown hair and a clever face: shrewd little black eyes with deep pouches under them, a sharp beak of a nose, and a long mouth.

'I've got it! Bromley. The men's outfitters. He's just opened a store in Frederick Street. You know the one. It cuts across Herriot Row.'

'How can I meet him? I can't spend too much time away from my station.'

'Trouble is, I don't know the man.'

'Can you find out where his office is?'

'Wait. I see Johnny Heather over there. He knows everyone and everything.'

David was gone only a few minutes.

'His office, as far as Johnny knows, is in his shop. He doesn't know the number of the shop but if you take a walk along Frederick Street, he says you can't miss it. What will you do?'

'I'll go and talk to him. Say I own fish farms in Canada and I am bursting with wealth to invest. See what happens. I might need to stay overnight.'

'I've got a wee flat in Abercrombie Place. I'll take you round there after lunch. You can use it if you're stuck in town. If the phone rings, don't answer it. It might be a lady.'

'Aha, that's why you've got a wee flat in town. Does the wife know?'

175

'God forbid.'

When lunch was over, they walked to Abercrombie Place. Hamish had brought an overnight bag just in case. David handed him the keys. 'Let's have a look at you again. Hamish, that's a cheap watch.'

'So? I'm an eccentric billionaire.'

'Borrow my Rolex and don't lose it. It's an oyster and you could buy a wee house for the price o' that. Good hunting and let me know how you get on.'

The day was fine. Hamish suddenly thought of Priscilla and wished they were walking together through this most beautiful of cities. Hard to imagine, here in the centre, that there were grim, crime-ridden housing estates on the outside of the charmed Georgian New Town.

He found the clothing store. The prices were very high. The name BROMLEY was in thick gold letters above the door. He pushed it open and walked in. A male assistant in a kilt of one of the gaudier tartans minced forward. 'Can I help you, sir?'

'Just looking around,' said Hamish. Because of the pads in his cheeks, his voice did not sound like his own.

'Do look at our new suede jackets,' urged the assistant. 'They're to die for.'

'I hear you've just opened,' said Hamish. 'I'm over from Canada and I'm looking for good investments. I heard Mr Bromley was a shrewd businessman. I just had lunch at the Merlin Club and his name was mentioned.'

'As a matter of fact, Mr Bromley is in his office. I'll call him.'

After a few minutes, Thomas Bromley bustled in, as fat and cheerful as Hamish remembered him, the smile on his small mouth, however, never reaching his watchful, assessing eyes. Like his assistant, he was dressed in a kilt and ruffled shirt under a velvet jacket. The kilt, reflected Hamish, only looked good when worn by sturdy men with good legs. Chubby as he was, Bromley had stick-like legs.

He rubbed his hands. 'I hear you are interested in investing. Why don't we go over to the pub and have a chat.' His eyes swept over Hamish's expensive suit and flicked a glance at the expensive Rolex on his wrist.

They walked to a pub and entered into the beer-smelling gloom. Hamish ordered whisky and Bromley said he would have the same.

'And who do I have the honour of addressing?' he asked.

'I'm Diarmuid Jenkins the Third,' said Hamish. 'My mother was Highland and my father was Canadian. I own several fish farms and other businesses. I always regard Scotland as my home country.'

'That's fine. Are you interested in the clothing business?'

'Not really. I was thinking more of something like the restaurant business.'

'Now, there's a thing. I happen to have an interest in restaurants. I am the main shareholder in a chain of them.'

'In Scotland?'

'Not yet. But thinking of expanding. My company is called Britfood. My restaurants are very successful. Look, a friend of mine has a better head for business than I have. Why don't we all meet up for dinner at the Merlin Club tonight and discuss things over a good bottle of wine? Say, eight o'clock?'

'I'd like that,' said Hamish. He gave a rather vacant laugh. 'Back home I've a good manager, although he annoys me by saying that if the running of things was left to me, we'd be broke tomorrow. I want to show him I can do things for myself.'

'That's the ticket!' said Bromley, rubbing his chubby hands. 'You'll show him by the time I'm finished with you.'

As he got ready for the evening, Hamish thought he would be glad when the masquerade was over. The pads in his cheeks were uncomfortable and the glasses were pinching his nose. He put on Priscilla's uncle's evening suit and set out for the Merlin Club, phoning Willie Lamont before he left to say that he'd been delayed.

He had not been frightened before in his dealings with Bromley, but when he walked into the club and saw Charles Prosser sitting there he suddenly felt a frisson of fear. His Highland sixth sense picked up danger. Prosser hailed him, all bluff and hearty and with a crushing handshake. Hamish proceeded to play the rather pompous idiot very well, carefully instilling into their brains that his excellent manager was the one with the business acumen. Then Prosser said, if 'Diarmuid' didn't mind, he had some papers to leave at his office. As they approached Prosser's office, Hamish noticed a burglar alarm box over the door. Bromley poured Hamish a drink from a bar in the corner. At one point, Prosser excused himself and opened a safe in the wall. Hamish had turned on a little tape recorder in his pocket and recorded the clicks.

'The best idea is for you to come round to my office tomorrow at noon,' said Prosser, putting some papers in the safe and shutting it again, 'and we can all go through the business then. Here's my card. But tonight's for fun.'

When they moved to a pub after dinner, Hamish insisted on buying the first round. He went up to the bar and ordered double whiskies for both men and then said to the barman, 'How would you like to serve me cold tea and keep the price of my drinks for yourself?'

'Right, mac. You're my man.'

Hamish then proceeded to pretend he was getting very drunk. He slurred that he was determined to return to Canada with a good portfolio and slam it down on the desk of his manager.

The evening finally broke up. Hamish insisted on walking and lurched off down the street.

Once back at the flat, he took the pads out of his cheeks, dressed in a black sweater and trousers, assembled a housebreaking tool kit, set the alarm for two in the morning, and fell asleep.

Tam Tamworth was trying to sleep in one of the spare bedrooms at Milly's house. Three times the evening before he had tried to summon up courage to propose marriage to Milly, but each time the words just wouldn't come.

Suddenly he sniffed the air. There was a smell of smoke. Maybe Milly had left a pot on the cooker. He wrapped himself in a voluminous dressing gown and made his way downstairs. The smell was coming from the drawing room. He flung open the door. Coals and wood were blazing on the floor in front of the fire. He rushed into the kitchen, ran a bucket of water, ran back to the drawing room, and threw the water over the fire. It took another bucket of water to put the fire out.

He stood looking down at the blackened mess, scratching his hair. It had been a warm evening, and they hadn't lit the fire.

Tam went up the stairs and opened the door of Milly's bedroom. He shook her awake. 'Did you light the fire, Milly?'

'What fire?'

'The drawing room.'

She struggled up against the pillows. 'No, Tam. What's up?'

'I'm getting the police. Someone tried to burn the house down.'

Milly put on her dressing gown and followed him downstairs. She let out a shriek of alarm when she saw the burned mess in the drawing room. Tam phoned Hamish but only got the answering service. He then phoned Strathbane. He was told to contact Hamish Macbeth but replied that he was not getting any answer from the police station at Lochdubh. Police Inspector Mary Benson was roused and told of the fire. She telephoned Jimmy Anderson and asked sharply where Hamish was. When he said he did not know, she told him to get over to Drim immediately. The Scenes of Crime Operatives were already on their way.

Milly sat in the kitchen waiting for them to arrive, her face white with shock. Tam went up to his room and collected the diamond engagement ring. He returned to the kitchen and knelt down in front of Milly and took her cold hands in his. He mutely held up the ring box and looked at her with pleading eyes.

Milly opened the box. 'Will you marry me?' asked Tam in a hoarse voice.

A faint pink suffused her pale cheeks and she said shyly, 'Oh, yes.'

He stood up and leaned forward to kiss her when there came a hammering at the door.

'Damn,' he muttered and went to answer it.

At first Hamish thought it was his alarm and then realized it was his mobile phone. Jimmy was at the other end. 'Where the hell are you? Someone tried to set the captain's house on fire.'

'Is Milly all right?'

'Yes, fortunately Tamworth was staying there and got the fire out in time. Why aren't you at the station?'

'I'll tell you when I get back. Cover for me. Tell them one of my family's been taken ill.'

'You're in Edinburgh, you daft loon!'

'Help me, Jimmy. I'll come back with the murderer.'

'This once. Just this once.'

Hamish made his way through the quiet streets. When he got to Prosser's office, he looked carefully to left and right but did not see anyone. He took out a bunch of skeleton keys and got to work. It took him half an hour to unlock the door. A burglar alarm let out a shrill noise. He wrenched open the control box and cut the wires. He had noticed earlier that fortunately there were no CCTV cameras covering the entrance. He sat and waited in case he heard the police arrive and had to make a quick getaway.

After a quarter of an hour, he entered Prosser's office. With a pencil torch between his teeth, he searched the desk but did not find anything incriminating. He went to the safe, took out his tape recorder, and listened to the clicks. It took him half an hour to get the right combination. The safe swung open. He found a file of letters, two thick ledgers, and piles of banknotes. He took out the ledgers and laid them on the desk. Here were lists of all the companies. He risked switching on an Anglepoise lamp. Taking out a camera, he photographed page after page. Then he opened the file of letters. There was one from the late Captain Davenport saying that he could make them all a fortune. He had employed a geologist, and rich seams of gold had been found in Perthshire. But he needed funding for mining equipment. He would put up most of the money himself but would need an extra £500,000 and in return he would make Prosser a majority shareholder. Hamish photographed that as well.

When he had finished, he returned everything to the safe. Before he closed the door, he stared at all that money. He took two plastic bags out of his pocket and stuffed both bags full. May as well make it look like a robbery, he thought, because Prosser would discover the wires on his burglar alarm had been cut.

He let himself out and walked back to the flat. What do I do now, he wondered. If I just disappear, they'll get hold of David Harrison and sweat my real identity out of him.

He phoned David Harrison. A sleepy David answered the phone. Hamish rapidly explained the situation. 'Could you and your family disappear for a week?' he asked.

'I was about to take a holiday. But why?'

'Because if I clear off, these villains will be after you to find out my real identity.'

'What an exciting life you do lead,' said David. 'But keep in touch. I'll want to know when it's safe to come back.'

'They're all in on it,' said Hamish. 'I was with Bromley and Prosser but one of the others must have gone to Drim and tried to set the captain's house on fire.'

Hamish snatched two hours' sleep and then packed up everything. He took the pads out of his cheeks and ripped off his fake moustache. He found a pair of sharp scissors and hacked off all his hair, then shaved his scalp. He

184

pulled his cap over his bald head and quietly let himself out. He hailed a passing taxi and asked to be driven to the airport, not relaxing until he saw Edinburgh disappearing under the plane's wings.

He took a taxi all the way from Inverness airport to Lochdubh, guiltily paying the fare with notes he had stolen from the safe, hoping they would not turn out to be forged.

Once more, he printed off his photographs on the machine in Patel's. Wearing gloves, he put the pile of photographs in a plain envelope. Then he drove to Strathbane.

Jimmy was sitting sleepily at his desk. 'I want you to say this lot landed on your desk and you don't know who gave them to you,' whispered Hamish. 'There's enough in there for you to pull Prosser in. Now go on as if you've summoned me and demand to know where the hell I was.'

'But I told them about a member of your family being ill!'

'Shout that you phoned my mother and that they were all well and call me a skiving bastard or something like that.'

Prosser strode up and down his office in a rage. 'Before I call the police,' he shouted at Bromley, 'take the ledgers and correspondence and lock them in your safe.'

'You can't phone the police,' said Bromley miserably.

'Why the hell not?'

'That money was never declared to the tax man. They'll ask questions about it.'

Prosser clutched his hair. 'Phone Sanders and Castle and get them here.'

'What about Diarmuid Jenkins?'

'He's due here soon. May as well see how much we can get out of him.'

By one o'clock, when Bromley had returned after putting the ledgers and correspondence in his safe, Prosser was beside himself with rage. 'He hasn't shown and David Harrison is nowhere to be found.'

Prosser went suddenly quiet. He sat down behind his desk. He said slowly, 'I think this Diarmuid is behind all this. Look, he chats us up, he says he's going to invest, and yet he doesn't turn up. I'm going to phone round all the hotels and see if I can trace him.'

But no hotel in Edinburgh had heard of Diarmuid Jenkins or had any guest answering his description.

By evening, Castle and Sanders arrived and learned about the robbery. 'Thank your stars it was just the money he was after,' said Sanders. 'Those ledgers are dynamite. Why the hell didn't you keep them in a safe-deposit box?'

'Why the hell don't you shut your mouth or I'll shut it for you permanently,' said Prosser.

They all started as a loud knocking came at

the street door and a stentorian voice shouted, 'Police! Open up!'

'We're blown,' said Prosser. 'Follow me.'

He pressed a button in the wood panelling, and a door slid open. They followed him down a narrow staircase that led into a weedy garden at the back. He opened a gate in the garden wall. Outside in the lane was parked a four-wheel drive. They all piled in and sped off.

'All gone,' said Jimmy wearily the next day when he called on Hamish. 'But we had search warrants for their offices. Prosser owned Scots Entertainment, not to mention other suspicious companies, and Bromley owns Timothy's in Guildford. But as to the murders, it's all too circumstantial. They hadn't time to clear out any of their bank accounts in this country, but they've probably got money stashed abroad. We hoped if we'd got them all that one of them would crack and turn Queen's evidence to get off.'

'I hate this Queen's evidence,' said Hamish. 'I remember a case where two boys murdered an old granny for the few coins in her purse. One held down her head while the other sawed it off. The one who'd held down her head turned Queen's evidence and walked free.'

'We've frozen their bank accounts,' said Jimmy.

Hamish sighed. 'They've probably got money all over the world. I wonder if we'll ever catch them. It was vanity on Prosser's part, keeping those accounts in his safe. I bet he liked to gloat over them. Then along comes Davenport and cons him out of a large chunk of money. There's no record of how much. I bet it was in cash, too.'

Chapter Ten

A direful death indeed they had
That would put any parent mad
But she was more than usual calm
She did not give a single damn
— MARJORY FLEMING

Angela Brodie sat miserably in front of a table of her books in a Glasgow bookshop. As she was damned as a literary writer, interest in her had flared and died even though her book reviews were excellent. In the past hour, she had only signed three books. To make matters worse, she had to share her signing with a well-known detective writer of the slash 'em, torture 'em, and sodomize 'em genre whose queue stretched out across the shop.

I've been nominated for the Haggart, thought Angela. My sales are respectable. I've got a contract to write two more. I think ambition is some sort of pernicious infection.

She looked up. A woman with a familiar face

was smiling down at her. 'Would you sign, please? Just your signature.'

Angela signed her name. 'Don't I know you?'

The woman leaned forward and whispered: 'I'm one of the booksellers. It's a shame there aren't more people.'

Oh, Hamish Macbeth, thought Angela. Lack of ambition is a truly good thing to have.

She suddenly gathered up her belongings and walked straight out of the bookshop, blinking in the sunshine of Buchanan Street. 'I'm going home,' she muttered. 'I'm going back to my old life.' A man eyed her nervously and gave her a wide berth.

Milly Davenport was working in the garden, humming a tune as she dug the spade into what was once a flower bed, determined to make it bloom again.

The phone in the house rang shrilly. Milly hesitated only a moment. Tam usually answered all calls for her. She ran to get it. An angry voice shouted down the line before she could even say, 'Hello.'

'Harcourt here,' said the voice. 'Look, Tam, we know you've been romancing thon widow woman for the background stuff but you're spending too much time in Drim and there's work to be done here. There was no need to actually get engaged to the woman. She could sue you for breach o' promise when she finds out you were just using her. Also, you missed the story about those four men fleeing the country. Get your sorry arse in gear now!'

The phone was slammed down at the other end.

Milly slowly replaced the receiver. She should have known, she thought. Never trust a reporter. She didn't know where Tam was. He had said he wouldn't be back until the following day.

She wearily walked back into the garden and picked up the spade. She would dig and dig, hoping the physical exercise would keep the tears at bay. She seized the spade and rammed it down into the soft earth. The spade struck something. She knelt down and, picking up a trowel, cleared away the earth, exposing the corner of an attaché case. She dug around it until she could pull it up. It was locked.

She took it into the kitchen and attacked the hasps with a hammer until she had broken them and opened the case. It was stuffed full of banknotes. With trembling fingers, she lifted them all out on to the kitchen table and began to count them. The notes amounted to nearly £780,000.

Milly stared at the money. She thought of her late bullying husband who had made her life a misery and then she thought of Tam's perfidy. Suddenly as cold as ice, she packed up the money. Then she went upstairs and packed two suitcases with her clothes. She went outside and filled in the hole where the attaché case had reposed and covered the raw earth with clods of grass and weeds. She returned to the house, took off her engagement ring, and left it on the kitchen table.

She then went out, locking the door behind her. She drove to Inverness airport where she bought herself a ticket to London.

Once in London, she booked into the Waldorf Hotel in Aldwych, then went to a travel agent and reserved a cabin on a Caribbean cruise liner due to leave Southampton the following day. She had not used the money in the suitcase . . . yet. That would do for spending money on board.

Tam was lying in his bed in his flat in Strathbane, nursing one of the worst hangovers he could ever remember having. He had been careful not to drink too much in Milly's company but he had run into some colleagues the night before and set out on a drinking spree.

His doorbell rang. With a groan, he struggled out of bed and went to open the door. A fellow reporter stood there.

'Where have you been?' he demanded. 'Harcourt's going apeshit. I heard him phone you at that widow woman's and give you a rocket.'

'But I wasnae there,' exclaimed Tam, who

suddenly felt as if the bottom had dropped out of his stomach. 'Did you hear what he said?'

'Oh, jist ranted on that he knew you were romancing the Davenport woman for a story and getting engaged to her was maybe going a bit far because she could sue you for breach o' promise. Something like that.'

Tam swore and clutched his aching head. 'It's nothing like that,' he howled. 'I've got to see her.'

'You'd better see Harcourt first if you want to keep your job.'

It was evening before Tam got to Drim. He found the door locked and let himself in with the key Milly had given him. He went into the kitchen. Milly's engagement ring sparkled up at him from the table. He sat down heavily. Harcourt had told him he had thought he was talking to Tam because Tam had always answered the phone.

It'll be all right, thought Tam desperately. I'll wait until she comes home and explain everything.

He waited and waited all the long night but Milly did not return.

A week later, on the terrace of a rented villa just outside Rio de Janiero, sat four wanted men with their wives. They had not wanted to bring their wives but Prosser said it would be dangerous to leave them behind in case one of them opened her big, silly mouth.

'The new passports should be ready today,' said Prosser.

'But we've already got good forgeries,' protested Ferdinand Castle.

'Better be on the safe side,' said Prosser.

Bromley shifted uneasily in his rattan chair. He wished he had given himself over to the police. The whole thing was a nightmare. Why had he let Prosser talk him into something so idiotic as trying to set Davenport's house on fire? Milly left the door open during the day, and he had hidden in one of the attics until nightfall. Why had he let Prosser dominate him and frighten him? If he turned Queen's evidence, then he might get a considerably reduced sentence. Maybe in one of those open prisons. He was tired of his nagging wife and frightened of Prosser.

It was Prosser's psychopathic vanity that had led them to exile in Brazil. He had tried to tell Prosser at one time to forget Davenport, but Prosser had said he wanted revenge.

Bromley miserably counted up the murders: Captain Davenport, the sweep, Philomena Davenport, Betty Close, and that prostitute. How had he ever become drawn into this web of murder and deceit? What if the SAS were sent to Brazil to seize them? They had bribed a fishing boat to take them to France and then journeyed overland by rented car to Lisbon, where they had booked flights to Rio. They had used cloned credit cards to pay for the rented car and their fares.

The thought of escape grew in his mind. At one point, he felt Prosser's bottle-green eyes fixed on him and threw the man a weak smile. Prosser held the cloned credit cards. If he escaped, he daren't pay the airfare with cash because that would ring alarm bells. But, he suddenly thought, a travel agent would be glad of the cash.

How to get away?

Charles Prosser said suddenly, 'Have you got that photo of Diarmuid whatsisname? I told the waiter to snap it and you kept a print.'

'I think it's in my case,' said Bromley.

'Go and get it.'

Bromley returned after some time and handed Prosser the photograph. He studied it, then brought out a magnifying glass and peered at it again.

He sat back in his chair, his face turning white with anger. 'I think that bastard was that Highland constable, Macbeth.'

Sanders let out a nervous laugh. 'Come on. That great idiot?'

'He was on television. He's solved a lot of murders. He was sniffing around Scots Entertainment and then John Dean reported he had called at the Canongate flat asking about Betty Close. I'll have that bastard.'

'You can't,' said Sanders gloomily. 'We daren't go back.'

'You can stay here. I'm getting even with that policeman if it's the last thing I do.'

'You'll get caught,' said Bromley.

'I won't. As soon as the new passports arrive, I'm off.'

'And what am I supposed to do?' asked Sandra petulantly.

'Take up knitting. I don't care.'

I have to get there before him, fretted Bromley. I know Prosser. If he gets caught, he'll take us all down with him. He may even try to pin the murders on one of us!

'I'm off to get the passports,' said Prosser, getting to his feet.

Now's my chance, thought Bromley desperately. He waited until Prosser had driven off. Sandra said she was going for a dip in the pool and the others said they would join her. 'Coming, Tom?' she asked.

'Not me. I think I'll have a bit of a siesta.'

Sandra Prosser turned on her road to the pool and watched Bromley walk into the house. Suddenly suspicious, she told the others to go ahead and then waited in the garden behind a stand of palm trees.

Soon she saw Bromley get into the old car he had bought and drive off. She took out the mobile phone her husband had bought her when they had arrived in Rio and spoke to him urgently.

Prosser, who had just collected the new passports, swore under his breath and headed for the airport.

There was a flight for London via Sao Paulo due to leave at seven o'clock that evening. He sat and waited.

Thomas Bromley also waited but in a bar facing Copacabana Beach. It was surrounded by a low hedge. Bands played outside and then stretched their hands over the hedge for payment. Little children often sneaked in around the tables, begging for money before being chased off by the waiter. He kept taking out his air ticket and looking at it to make sure it was really there.

The sun beat down. Tall Brazilian girls wearing the minimum of beachwear strolled past on very high heels. He had noticed that some of them even did their shopping in the town wearing only thongs and tiny scraps of material over their firm breasts.

He rose at last and found a taxi to take him to the airport. He had left his car in a back street.

Prosser was wearing a baseball cap pulled down over his face and dark glasses. He had changed his clothes and was wearing a Hawaiian shirt and Bermuda shorts and trainers. Bromley did not recognize him. The flight was called. With a beating heart, he boarded the plane and, with a great sigh of relief, took his seat in first class. He had paid for his seat with cash but at the airport had used his genuine passport. That way, he would be picked up by the police at Heathrow.

As the flight raced along the runway for take-off, Prosser in the seat behind Bromley lifted his shirt and ripped off a syringe of morphine he had taped to his body. He had been grateful that new security X-ray machines had not been installed at Rio. The syringe was plastic and so had not been detected. There was no one sitting next to him. He waited patiently during the long journey. As they approached Heathrow for the landing and the airline crew retired to put on their seat belts, Prosser leaned forward. Between a gap in the seats, he could see Bromley's arm on the armrest. He plunged the syringe into it. Bromley let out a strangled cry that was drowned by the roar of the engines as the plane landed.

As he left the plane, Prosser glanced down at Bromley. To all intents and purposes, it looked as if he were asleep. It would take several days for them to find out that Bromley had not died of natural causes. It never crossed his mind that Bromley would have used his real passport.

Angela Brodie found that returning to her old life was difficult. Although she had carefully avoided basing any one of her characters on the people in Lochdubh, the villagers were convinced that this one and that one was really old so-and-so. The villagers were deadly polite to her, a particularly Highland way of sending someone to Coventry.

Her husband was unsympathetic. 'You should never have done it, Angela,' he said, but as her eyes filled with tears, he said, 'Oh, look, let's go to the hotel for dinner tonight and the hell with the lot of them.'

Angela felt a wave of great affection for her husband as they sat down for dinner. Not once had he shouted at her. He had been puzzled at first as to why she would do such a thing as use a thinly disguised village of Lochdubh as a basis for her novel, but then had accepted the fact that his surprising wife was a brilliant woman.

'Oh, look!' exclaimed Angela. 'There's Priscilla. I wonder if Hamish knows.'

The tall blonde figure of Priscilla had just entered the dining room. She saw them and came to join them. 'And how's the famous author?' she asked.

'Being sent to Coventry by the locals,' said Angela.

'They'll get over it,' said Priscilla. 'There might be a quick way to do it.'

'How?'

'Give six free writing classes on the theme of How to Write About What You Know. They'll come along because it's free. Throw in some tea and cakes as well.'

'It wasn't a success when that horrible television scriptwriter gave classes,' pointed out Dr Brodie.

'But he was awful and it turned out he was a plagiarist who couldn't write.'

Angela brightened. 'It might work.'

'What did Hamish think about being portrayed as the local Lothario?' asked Priscilla.

'He was annoyed, poor man. But you know Hamish. He never bears a grudge.'

'Well . . .' Priscilla was about to point out that Hamish was a Highlander, a race capable of bearing grudges until the end of time, but decided to say instead, 'If there's anything I can do to help set up your classes, let me know.'

She smiled down at the obviously devoted couple and wondered how she could ever have believed Hamish guilty of having an affair with Angela. She said good evening to them and then drove to the police station.

Hamish's face lit up in a glad smile when he opened the door to her, a smile to be quickly replaced with a look of caution. He did not want to be hurt again.

'Come ben,' he said. 'What brings you north?'

'A holiday owing.'

'Didn't the Australian job work out?'

200

'It was a contract computer job that ran its course. I'll start again in London when my agency finds me something. Now, let's sit down and you can tell me all your news.'

Hamish began at the beginning, telling her the latest disturbing news that Bromley had been found dead on a plane at Heathrow. As he had used a genuine passport, police had figured that he meant to turn himself in – but someone had followed him on to the plane. 'The UK has an extradition treaty with Brazil so we hope the Brazilian police are rounding up the rest of them.'

But Sandra had received a call from her husband at Heathrow. 'Get out of there,' Prosser had said. 'Bromley's taking a plane to London and he's going to betray all of us.'

Meaning you, Sandra had thought, numb with shock. The fact that her husband was a serial killer finally hit her. Why should she run like a fugitive? She had access to her husband's money squirrelled away in the Cayman Islands. She had done nothing wrong. She could hear the others talking on the terrace, wondering where Prosser and Bromley had got to. Why should she care what happened to Castle, Sanders, and their wives?

She had no intention of being dragged off to some smelly Brazilian cell. Her husband would have used one of the new fake passports. She would have to pray the old fake passport still worked.

Sandra opened the safe in the villa and pulled out wads of banknotes along with several bank books. She stripped naked and Sellotaped the money to her body before dressing again. She did not want to risk packing or calling for a taxi. It was going to be a long hot walk into town.

Chapter Eleven

A man that studieth revenge keeps his own wounds green.

— FRANCIS BACON

'I don't think Prosser will go back to Brazil,' said Hamish. 'I don't think he cares what happens to anyone other than himself. Keeping those ledgers was an act of supreme vanity. So what's the next move of a man with supreme vanity?'

'Disappear to some country where they don't have extradition,' suggested Priscilla. She was wearing a blue cotton shirtwaister, as blue as her eyes. The shining bell of her hair fell evenly on either side of her calm face. Hamish felt a treacherous tug of attraction but mentally shrugged it off.

'If Prosser thinks the mysterious Diarmuid is me, then he'll come after me. He will see me as the ruin of his life. He will want to get even before he disappears. There were few passengers in first class, and the one seated behind

Bromley answering to the name of Higgins fits the description of Prosser.'

Priscilla looked alarmed. 'Have you told Strathbane about your suspicions?'

'I tried. But Blair blocked it. He's probably praying that I'm right.'

'Take a holiday,' urged Priscilla.

'No, I think I'll chust bide here,' said Hamish, the sudden strengthening of his accent showing he was not as calm as he was trying to be. 'But there's one thing you could do for me.'

'What's that?'

'Take my dog and cat up to the hotel and get chef Clarry to take care of them for a bit. I don't want Prosser poisoning them before he comes for me.'

'And you're just going to stay here like a tethered goat?'

'That's me,' said Hamish with a grin and then bleated.

But an unusually fine summer finally went out in a blaze of glory with purple burning on the flanks of the mountains and there had been no attempt on Hamish's life.

Sanders, Castle, and their wives were still in prison in Brazil, awaiting extradition. They had sung like canaries to visiting detectives from Scotland Yard. The hunt for Prosser and his wife was worldwide. Photographs of what they looked like and what they might look like if they had changed their hair colour and donned disguises had appeared on television and in all the papers.

Angela's writing classes had been a great success, and budding authors tapped away at computers. There was the usual weekly ceilidh at the village hall. Lochdubh had returned to normal for everyone but Hamish Macbeth. Priscilla had left to take up a new contract but occasionally phoned Hamish to make sure he was well.

Elspeth phoned as well and said she might come up on a week's holiday.

Hamish diligently checked the background of any visitor to Lochdubh. He was still convinced that Prosser was plotting his revenge. The man might not come in person, he reasoned, but send someone else after him.

Sandra, by dint of remembering the name of the man her husband was going to see about fake passports, had finally run him to earth in the back streets of Rio. Before that, she had gone to a beauty salon and had her hair cut and dyed black. The forger demanded a lot of money and to his delight, Sandra did not even bother to haggle. She even said she would pay more for a rush job. So she sat and waited while he worked, hoping that her husband had not told any of the others the man's name in case they found her. She did not want to be encumbered by anyone.

At last, the passport was ready. She got the forger to give her a lift into the centre of town, where she bought some clothes and a suitcase before catching a cab to the airport.

Despite the air conditioning in the airport, she was sweating profusely with nerves as she approached passport control. When her passport was finally stamped after what seemed a terrifying age, she felt limp with relief. She had bought a ticket to Sao Paulo. She studied the destination boards at the airport and then bought a ticket to Santiago in Chile. When she arrived at Santiago airport, she went to a tourist desk and booked a hotel in the city, then picked up a cab.

The hotel was dated and somehow very dark. The furnishings were old-fashioned Spanish, and in her room the windows were covered with lace under heavy velvet curtains. She stripped off and laid the notes on the bed. She decided she had to find some other way of carrying them because if she sweated any more, the notes might be damaged. Several packets had actually become detached from the Sellotape and fallen inside her blouse.

She went out for a walk on O'Higgins Boulevard, feeling lonely and threatened by the crowds. She planned to keep moving from place to place until she felt safe. She bought a small travel bag in a shop and then realized she was hungry.

Sandra went into a restaurant on the boulevard. There was a list of dishes all in Spanish. A waiter approached her table but did not speak English. Sandra's stomach rumbled. She had been too nervous to eat anything since she began her flight. A handsome young man at the next table stood up and said in perfect English, 'May I help you?'

Sandra smiled at him. 'I can't read the menu.'

'They serve very good roast pork here.'

'I'll have that, and some wine.' Loneliness bit at Sandra again. 'Why don't you join me?'

He sat down, and soon they were laughing and talking. He said he was a student, studying medicine. His name was Jaime. He had curly black hair, large brown eyes fringed with black lashes, and a slim figure.

Sandra said grandly that she was travelling the world. He suggested afterwards that they go on to a bar but Sandra wanted to change into something attractive and repair her make-up. She loved the way he smiled into her eyes, banishing her fears of the police, making her feel young again. He escorted her back to her hotel, a supportive hand under her arm, and said he would wait for her in reception.

In her room, Sandra washed her face and carefully applied make-up. She studied herself critically in the bathroom mirror. Her figure was still good, and her siliconed breasts were holding up. She thought the dark hair suited her. Out of her meagre supply of clothes, she picked out a blue cotton shift dress and slipped on a pair of high-heeled sandals. She had hidden the money under the mattress. She took it out and stuffed it into the travel bag. It was then Sandra hesitated. She really should put it in the hotel safe, but she did not trust the staff.

She put it on top of the huge old-fashioned wardrobe and went down to meet her date.

She spent a drunken, riotous evening and ended up in bed with Jaime.

Jaime lay awake while Sandra snored beside him. He planned to ask her for money. He wasn't a student but worked as a waiter in the evenings and as a deliveryman for a clothing factory during the day. On his odd evenings off, he searched for rich tourists, sometimes being successful enough to get money for his services in bed.

They had left the lights on. Sandra's suitcase was lying open. He slid quietly out of bed. It contained very little. He wondered whether to take money from her handbag and then decided it might be more profitable to work on her. If she fell in love with him, she might fund him to go to medical school, which had always been his dream.

He got back into bed and was about to fall asleep when he noticed the travel bag perched on top of the wardrobe. She had obviously just bought it when he met her in the restaurant. He got up again, stood on a chair, lifted down the bag from the wardrobe, climbed down holding the bag, and placed it on the floor.

Jaime opened it and suppressed a gasp as he saw all that money. He thought of his ambitions to be a doctor; he thought of his family out in the squalid barrio. He quietly closed the bag, and with his heart thudding so loudly that he was afraid Sandra would wake up, he quickly dressed, let himself out of the room, and then made his escape through a fire door at the end of the corridor.

Tam Tamworth haunted Drim but there was no sign of Milly. He longed for her to come back so that he could tell her he really loved her.

The summer was gone and a cold wind was blowing down from the mountains. The restless seagulls wheeled overhead as he trudged away from the house. He knew he should return to Strathbane. He was supposed to be out following up a tip-off about a drugs raid. He had found out quickly that it was a fiction from some unreliable informant but had not informed the news desk, using the time instead to search for Milly.

He decided to go for a walk up on the moors, wondering, always wondering, where she had gone and if she ever thought of him.

Tam had gone a good way from Drim. He stood on an outcrop of rock, looking down at the village, thinking it would be marvellous if he could see her car drive up.

And then he saw a figure, made small by the distance, leaving the back of the house.

'Hey!' he called, but his voice was whipped away with the wind. He started to run back down to the village, stumbling and cursing. When he reached the house, he checked round it but could not see anyone; nor was there any sign of a break-in.

He took out his phone and called Hamish.

'I'll be right over,' said Hamish.

'I can't wait for you,' said Tam. 'I'm supposed to be at the office. Phone me if you catch him.'

Hamish drove quickly to Drim. Like Tam, he searched around the house and checked the locks. Then he took out a pair of powerful binoculars and scanned the moors. No one.

He was suddenly sure it was Prosser at last.

Sandra awoke in the morning and stretched luxuriously. She turned and felt for Jaime and found the bed empty. She looked up at the wardrobe and saw immediately that the bag was missing.

Sheer panic gripped her, followed by white-hot rage. She rose and dressed hurriedly. She was relieved to find there was still a wad of notes in her handbag. Sandra felt murderous. She went down to reception and asked at the desk if someone could translate for her for a small fee. A girl was summoned. Her English was not very good but Sandra felt sure it would be good enough for her purpose.

They walked together to the restaurant, where Sandra gave the girl a description of Jaime and said they had been dining together the evening before and she wanted to find him.

She gloomily expected to be told to come back later when the waiter who had served them would be on duty but the girl, after questioning the staff, said that Jaime worked at the Chile Modes clothing company. Sandra asked for the address and waited impatiently. The girl finally came back with a slip of paper with the address on it. Sandra tipped her and walked with her back to the hotel, where she bought a map of the city.

She then wandered down the boulevard until she found a shop selling tourist souvenirs. Sandra bought a baseball cap and then saw they had a display of souvenir knives. She bought the one with the longest blade.

Returning to the hotel, she asked the concierge to hire her a car, asking for a four-wheel drive as she said she would like to see some of the country. When she paid for the hire and deposit, she had very little money left.

In Guildford, Sandra had taken the advanced driving test. She had often driven her husband when they were abroad on holidays. The car had a satnav, so she followed the directions and soon found herself in an industrial park on the outskirts of the city.

Chile Modes was in a low building at the back of the estate. She sat and waited, watching small delivery vans come and go, the new baseball cap pulled down over her eyes. Her heart sank as she realized that Jaime had probably disappeared with the money. He would expect her to have called the police.

But suddenly she saw Jaime emerge from the building, and he was carrying her travel bag. He was shouting something at a burly man and then gave him the finger.

Jacking in his job, thought Sandra, with a rising feeling of excitement. Jaime got on to a battered Vespa after strapping the travel bag to the back of the seat. She ducked down as he roared past her. Sandra swung the car round and followed in pursuit. She hoped he would not go back into the centre of the city – following a Vespa, which could nip in and out of the heavy traffic, would be difficult – but he drove off into the countryside along a dusty road. The magnificence of the Andes loomed in the distance.

She looked cautiously in her rear-view mirror. Apart from the two of them, the road was empty. Sandra put her foot down on the accelerator, raced forward, swerved as she came alongside him, and sent him flying into the ditch, where he lay stunned.

She got down from her vehicle. Quickly she unstrapped the travel bag and threw it into her car. Jaime came stumbling up on to the road. He drew a knife out of his boot. His eyes were gleaming with rage. Sandra thought of prison and all because of this idiot. He brandished the knife.

'Give me the money,' he said.

'All right,' said Sandra with deceptive mild-ness. She leaned into the car but picked up a tyre iron, thinking quickly that if she engaged in a knife fight with Jaime, she would lose. She threw the bag in his face and then lunged for-ward and smashed the tyre iron down on his head with all her force.

Then she stood back, panting, looking des-perately to right and left. His head was a mass of blood. She forced herself to feel for a pulse but found none. Sandra put down the back seats in the car and, with a superhuman effort, shoved his body in.

Heading towards the city, she stopped at a wayside stall that was selling shawls and bought two. She covered Jaime's body and drove off. Now the problem was to dump the body somewhere it wouldn't be found until she was well clear of the country.

She passed a tavern that was little more than a shack; a little farther on was a building site. The men must be on their break. They had been laying the foundations of a building and cement had been poured into an oblong square, shaded with a plastic covering on poles.

Sandra got out. She knelt down and felt the cement. It was wet. She dragged the body out of the car and tumbled it into the cement. Would it be deep enough? Jaime lay lifeless, and then the body slowly disappeared from view.

Spotting a barrel of water at the side with a ladle next to it, she ladled a scoop of water over the cement to smooth out any disturbance on the surface. It wasn't perfect but she hoped the workers would think they'd made a sloppy job or that some animal had fallen in.

Sandra wasn't worried about the Vespa. She shrewdly guessed that someone would steal it before nightfall.

When she returned to the hotel, after scrubbing out the inside of the car and then taking it through a car wash, she checked out.

As she drove steadily north out of Santiago, she suddenly remembered her husband saying, 'What I like about you, Sandra, is that you're as bad as me.' She hadn't known what he had meant. Now she did.

* * *

214

A week later, Tam received a phone call from Ailsa. 'Milly's back,' she said.

'I'll be right there,' he cried.

'Don't! There's something you don't know,' cried Ailsa, but Tam had already slammed down the phone.

He bought a large bouquet of roses and headed out to Drim. Smoke was rising from the chimney. He knocked at the door.

Milly answered it. Her eyes widened when she saw him. 'Why, Tam . . .'

'Who is it?' called a male voice.

'Go away,' hissed Milly. A man appeared behind her. He was tall and middle-aged with thick grey hair and a pugnacious face. 'Who is this?' he demanded.

'An old friend of mine, Tam Tamworth,' said Milly. She raised a hand to brush a strand of hair away from her face, and the sun sparkled on a large diamond ring on her engagement finger.

'Come in, Tam,' said Milly. He gave her the roses.

He followed her into the kitchen. 'This is my fiancé, Giles Brandon,' said Milly in a low voice. 'We got engaged when I was on a cruise.'

Giles put an arm around Milly's shoulders. 'We're getting married as soon as possible. Milly wants to get married here.'

Tam wanted to shout that Milly was engaged

to him but there was something in her pleading, frightened eyes that stopped him.

'Don't just stand there, Milly,' said Giles.
'Make us some coffee.'

'It's all right,' said Tam. 'I'm off.'

He walked down to the village store. 'I tried
to stop you,' said Ailsa sadly. 'They arrived
yesterday, and, och, he's as bad a bully as the
captain was. She was only in the shop a few
minutes. She tried to pretend it was the great
romance but he came shoving in and said,
"Shouldn't you be getting my dinner instead
of standing here gossiping?"'

'I've got to talk to her in private,' said Tam.

'I've an idea,' said Ailsa. 'Get yourself over
to Lochdubh and get Hamish to ask that
Giles call at the police station. He'll think of
something.'

Hamish listened as Tam poured out his woes.

'So you really do love her?' said Hamish.
'It's not chust for a story?'

'I'd do anything to get her back.'

'I think Prosser's in the neighbourhood and
looking for a chance to get his revenge on
me,' said Hamish. 'I'll see if I can get Brandon
over here.'

Hamish phoned and spoke to Giles
Brandon. He said that a killer was stalking the
area, and he feared Milly might be in danger.
He suggested that Mr Brandon should come

216

to the police station immediately so that they could discuss security measures.

'Can't you come over here?' demanded Giles.

'There are some papers you need to see.'

'Oh, very well.' He hung up.

'I've got to go to the police station in Lochdubh, Milly,' Giles told her. 'Some bollocks about security. That man Prosser who's on the run wouldn't dare show his face in Scotland. These local yokels do panic. In my regiment, we didn't run from anyone. And when I get back, we'll go to an estate agent and put this place on the market.'

'Couldn't we stay?' asked Milly timidly. 'I like it here.'

'You don't know what's good for you. Stuck up here in the back of beyond! Just leave everything to me. Got it?'

He loomed over her, and she cringed back in her chair. 'Yes, dear.'

'That's the ticket. Won't be long.'

When he had gone, Milly thought miserably of how tender and caring he had been on the cruise. But when they had become engaged and got back to Britain, he had revealed himself to be a bully. She hadn't told him about the money she had found. She had been frightened he would tell her to hand it over to the police and so she put it back in her late husband's attaché case and reburied it in the flower bed.

* * *

Tam waited on the waterfront until he saw Brandon arrive at the police station and then roared off to Drim.

When Milly answered the door, Tam cried, 'Oh, Milly, why did you go away without telling me?'

'I overheard that phone call from your editor,' said Milly. 'It was plain you were just using me.'

'I wasn't,' said Tam desperately. 'I do love you, Milly, but I've got to keep up a front with the editor that I'm a hard-nosed reporter. If I told him the truth, he'd have stopped me spending so much time with you.'

'It's too late now,' said Milly. 'Go away. Don't make trouble for me.' And then she shut the door.

Prosser lay up on the moors. With a pair of powerful binoculars, he picked out the press card on the windscreen of Tam's car. Bloody reporters. But whoever that man was who was staying with Milly had to be got rid of. Then he would deal with Hamish Macbeth. After that, he would sweat Milly to find out where the missing money was. Davenport had been paid in cash. He would tie her up and take the house apart from top to bottom if she really didn't know where the money was.

He had seen the man drive off from the

house. He swallowed a couple of painkillers. His head ached abominably these days.

Prosser picked up his rifle and made his way down to the one-track Drim road.

Giles Brandon was feeling mellow. He considered Hamish Macbeth an overanxious fool, but a hospitable one at that. Seemingly not caring about the laws of drinking and driving, Hamish had plied him with a very fine old malt and deferred to his Army experience. Brandon had told him that he had recently retired. He had been a colonel and had served in Iraq.

He was halfway to Drim when he was stopped by a flock of sheep across the road. He peered around angrily looking for a shepherd but could see no one. The fine day had gone, and a damp drizzle was whipping across the heather. His pleasant mood gone, he slammed his hand impatiently on the horn. A few sheep scattered, but the rest looked at him with mild eyes.

Brandon got down from the car and waved his arms. 'Shoo!' he yelled. 'Bugger off!'

A bullet took him in the back of the head and he fell face down amongst the sheep. Prosser stepped forward and fired another two bullets into the back of his head.

Unaware that he was, in a way, imitating his wife, he dragged the body and dumped it into the back of Brandon's Land Rover. He got into the driver's seat and drove off across the heather, bumping along until he came to a heathery track. The sun had come out again, and everything glittered in the light. He went on up to the lip of a tarn, one of those little round lochs of Sutherland. Leaving the hand-brake off, he got down, went round the back of the vehicle, and began to push with all his might. At last, the Land Rover began to move. Over the edge it went, straight down into the water. There was an almighty splash and then silence. He leaned over the edge. Nothing now to be seen but a few ripples.

He was tired of sleeping rough. He was determined to find some shelter and wait until dark.

Milly waited and waited for Brandon to come back and, as the light began to fade, she phoned Hamish.

'I'm sure he'll be all right,' said Hamish. 'Give it a bittie longer.' But when he rang off, he thought guiltily of all the whisky he had given Brandon. He drove off towards Drim very slowly searching to right and left in case the man had driven off the road. Halfway along it, a shepherd, Terry McGowan, called on him to stop.

'What's up?' asked Hamish.

'Some bastard's cut my fences and I found my sheep all ower the road.'

Hamish climbed down from the Land Rover. It was not unknown for a rival crofter to cut another's fences, although it hadn't happened for a long time. Could it have been done to make Brandon stop? And if so, why? Was he connected in any way to Prosser? 'I'll look into it,' he said. He walked along the road for a bit, scanning the ground for any signs of an attack. But it was getting dark and although he shone a powerful torch this way and that, he could not see any signs of anything sinister.

He got back into his vehicle and went on to Drim. Milly had seen him coming and came out to meet him.

'Can't see him anywhere,' said Hamish. 'You go back in the house. I'm just going to put a call through to headquarters.'

He reported the missing Brandon and said he would need some men to help him search. He waited hopefully, but it was Jimmy Anderson who finally got back to him. 'No go,' he said. 'Blair says the man's probably off shopping in Inverness or somewhere.'

'Are that lot back from Brazil yet?'

'Yes, they're in Wormwood Scrubs on remand.'

'Get Scotland Yard to ask them if a Giles Brandon was involved in any of their crooked deals.'

'Hamish, I don't usually agree with Blair, but you know you should wait a bit or you'll look a right fool when he walks back in the door of Milly's house.'

Angus Macdonald, the seer, awoke suddenly that night. He sensed someone outside. He got slowly out of bed without putting on the light, unlocked the gun cabinet, and took out his shotgun. He deftly loaded it and went into his kitchen at the back of his cottage. He cautiously opened the back door, raised his shotgun, and fired it out into the blackness.

Prosser cursed and ran for cover. He had picked out the seer's cottage, hoping to break in and terrify some householder into giving him shelter until the small hours of the morning.

Angus phoned Hamish Macbeth. Hamish had been asleep, but he jumped out of bed as soon as Angus told him about the prowler.

Prosser, thought Hamish. He knew if he tried to get some manpower over, Blair would block it. He quickly dressed, ran to the church, and began to ring the bell.

The villagers began to gather in the church. Some of the old people remembered when the bell had been rung during the Second World War to alert them that a German warship had been spotted by one of the fishing boats.

Hamish decided to say that he thought the prowler was Prosser. When they had all gathered, he said, 'Thon murderer, Prosser, is on the loose around the village. I want you men to get your guns and spread out and hunt him down!'

High up above the village, Prosser stared down through his night-vision binoculars. He saw people streaming out of the church. Then he began to see men with guns beginning to leave the village and head up on to the moors.

He thought quickly. The safest place for him that night would be in the village itself. He would break into one of the cottages while the men were searching the moors and mountains for him, hold up some householder, and wait until the hunt had died down. Then he would take care of Hamish Macbeth.

The Currie sisters returned to their cottage on the waterfront. 'I'll make us a nice cup of cocoa,' said Nessie, 'after we've got into something comfortable.'

'Comfortable,' repeated her sister, the echo.

Nessie went into the kitchen and turned on the radio. She was getting rather deaf, and whistles and static sounded round the kitchen as she tried to find a programme with some music. At last, the music of the Polonaise from Eugene Onegin blasted round the kitchen.

The kettle had just boiled when Nessie felt something pressed against the side of her neck and a man's voice said, 'This is a gun. I have tied the other old bird up. One squeak out of you and I'll kill you both. Make me something to eat.'

Nessie, a small figure wrapped in a fluffy pink dressing gown, with old-fashioned steel rollers in her white hair, said, 'Bacon and eggs?'

'That'll do. I've cut the phone line so don't be getting any ideas. I'm going back into your living room and if you make a wrong move, I will shoot your friend.'

Nessie felt a dead calm. She took down a frying pan, opened the fridge, took out eggs and bacon, and then began to cook them. As if moving in a dream, she took down another pan and filled it up with bleach. She put two teabags into a teapot and then poured the boiling bleach in on top of them.

She slipped a sharp knife into her dressing-gown pocket. When everything was ready, she loaded up a large tray and carried it into the living room. Jessie stared at her, her eyes wide and blank with shock. She had tape over her mouth. Her ankles were bound with her dressing-gown cord.

Nessie put the tray down on the table by the window. Prosser looked a sinister figure. His face was blacked, and his clothes were filthy from sleeping rough.

He waved the pistol. 'You sit down while I eat,' he snarled. 'Pour the tea.'

Nessie poured him a large mug of tea. She sat down, back erect, and watched him in silence.

'Cut the bacon,' he snarled. He planned to eat with one hand while keeping the revolver levelled on her. Nessie cut the bacon into small pieces. She had covered the already salty bacon in salt.

He took a large gulp of tea, and his eyes bulged. He gasped and retched, clutching his throat. Nessie seized the pistol. But she knew nothing about guns and did not know how to release the safety catch. Prosser staggered to the door. All he wanted to do was get away. He crashed out into the night.

Nessie took out her knife and freed her sister. 'We've got to ring the bell,' she said. 'We've got to get the men back.'

'Mmm,' said Jessie, her mouth still covered by duct tape.

Up on the moors, Hamish and the searching men heard the bell. Cursing, Hamish sprinted down towards the village, his dog and cat at his heels.

In the church, in the corner where the bell rope of the single bell hung down, stood Nessie Currie, pulling on the rope for all she was worth.

When he tapped her on the shoulder, she screamed until she saw who it was.

The villagers were all crowding back into the church. Matthew Campbell, editor of the *Highland Times*, listened as Nessie told her story. Then, led by Hamish, they all ran out again to look for Prosser. Hamish stopped on the way and roused Jimmy. From Nessie's description, he said, it looked as if Prosser had come back to exact revenge.

All that night, the villagers, reinforced by police, searched all around while a police helicopter buzzed overhead.

The rain had cleared and the first Sutherland frost glittered on the heather. Lying buried in the heather, Prosser felt deadly ill. He would need to get back to Edinburgh, where he knew a doctor who owed him a favour. They would have roadblocks up all over the place. But he had to move or he would freeze to death. He daren't even go back to the bothie where he had hidden his rifle and other equipment.

He rose stiffly. His mouth was burning. A sheer desire to stay alive drove him up to his feet.

By a long circuitous route he arrived at the back of the Tommel Castle Hotel. The kitchen door was only a simple Yale lock, and he sprang it easily. He took a pencil torch out of his pocket and flashed it around the kitchen. He opened the fridge, took out a bottle of milk, and gulped as much down as he could. He ate dry bread and then drank more milk. Then he made his way quietly up the back stairs. He found an empty hotel room, the door standing open. He went in and shut and locked the door, first hanging a DO NOT DISTURB sign outside. Prosser stripped off and showered, tumbled into bed, and fell fast asleep.

When he awoke next morning, he decided he needed a change of clothes. He heard voices in the corridor outside as the guests went down for breakfast. He heard the people in the room next door, talking loudly as they walked away. Wrapped in a towelling robe he had found in the bathroom, he waited until the corridor was silent. He saw a maid coming along with clean sheets and positioned himself outside the door next to his.

'I'm afraid I've lost my key,' he said. He winked at her. 'I was just . . . er . . . visiting a friend.' The Polish maid giggled. She was new and had just come on duty. She smiled and opened the door with her pass key. She went to the door of the room he had spent the night in.

'Just leave her,' said Prosser. 'She wants to sleep until late.'

He went quickly into the room the maid had opened for him.

He opened drawers and took out clean underwear and put it on. It was a little bit large for him. He then opened the wardrobe and selected moleskin trousers, a hunting jacket, and a plaid shirt. He grinned. There was even a deerstalker. He crammed it down on his head.

Then he saw that the man had left his wallet on the bedside table. He snatched it up. He coolly walked out and down into reception and out into the car park. He got into the nearest car, one the hotel kept for guests, planning to hotwire it, but grinned when he saw the keys in the ignition.

By producing the driving licence he had found in the stolen wallet, he sailed through the roadblock. It was an old licence, the kind that did not have a photograph. Once the euphoria of escape left him, he realized he was running a temperature and felt very sick indeed. And yet he knew he would have to ditch the car and steal another. Any minute now, the hunt would be on for whoever had stolen the hotel guest's wallet and clothes along with one of the hotel cars.

He took the cash out of the wallet and then threw the wallet out of the window. He still had plenty of cash of his own but, he reflected, it was as well to have as much as he could get. He stopped in Dingwall. He felt dizzy and faint. He bought a new set of clothes and changed in a public toilet. Leaving the clothes he had stolen in the car, he hotwired a different vehicle he found parked in a far corner where he hoped it would be out of sight of any CCTV cameras.

He then drove to Inverness airport, where he left the car. He had one fake credit card left. He did not want to use it but knew he would have to risk it. Paying for an air ticket with cash might start alarm bells ringing.

When he arrived at Edinburgh airport, he felt dizzy. Summoning all his energies, he took a cab to the doctor's, burning with fever and thoughts of revenge.

Chapter Twelve

And come he slow, or come he fast,
It is but Death who comes at last.

— SIR WALTER SCOTT

A month of frantic searching for Prosser followed. Blair, beside himself with rage, tried to blame Hamish Macbeth, and Hamish Macbeth only, for having let the man get away.

The Currie sisters were not much good as witnesses. Lauded in the press as heroines, they told a story that became ever more elaborate, while their description of Prosser grew more weird and wonderful.

There was a police guard on Milly's house for two weeks until an impatient Daviot called it off, saying it was a waste of police time.

Despite frequent visits from Ailsa and other villagers, Milly felt very alone. The long, dark winter nights, and days where one hardly ever saw the sun added to her terror. She felt she should get away but on the other hand, where would she find such loyal friends as she had in Drim?

Her thoughts turned frequently to Tam. Had he loved her after all? How on earth could she have been so stupid as to nearly marry another bully?

Then one morning, she heard the sound of a vehicle arriving. She ran to the window and relaxed when she saw the familiar police Land Rover from Lochdubh. Then as the door on the passenger side of the Land Rover opened and the interior light of the vehicle came on, she saw Tam Tamworth getting out. She opened the door. Tam was standing there, looking sheepish. Hamish Macbeth said, 'Let us in, Milly. We've got something to discuss with you.'

In the kitchen, Hamish took off his hat and placed it on the table. His thick flaming red hair had grown back to its old length.

'It's like this, Milly,' began Hamish. 'Tam here really does love you. You need protection. I have a feeling that Prosser believes the money the captain took from him is still in this house. You didn't find any sign of anything?'

'No,' said Milly, standing with her back to him at the kitchen counter and plugging in the kettle.

Hamish eyed her suspiciously. If ever a back could lie, he thought, it was Milly's.

'If you do find the money,' he said, 'you must turn it over to the authorities and get

Tam here to write up the story. Prosser will see it and he will no longer have any reason to come after you.'

'I'll let you know if I find anything,' said Milly. 'Coffee?'

'Grand. Now, I think you should let Tam move in here. He's got holiday owing and he's prepared to spend it looking after you. What do you say?'

Milly placed a jug of coffee on the table and then three cups. 'Yes,' she said in a low voice. 'That would be fine. Is there no news at all of Giles?'

'Not a thing. It's my belief Prosser waylaid him, wanting him out of the way. I've asked again and again for the tarns and bogs to be searched but every time they turn me down. Hasn't he any family? I think the police asked you that and you said you didn't know but no one has come forward asking for him. He hadn't been married and his parents are dead. We can find no record of brothers or sisters.'

'I had begun to get the feeling he wasn't very popular,' said Milly. 'He was always running down people in his old regiment.'

'I'll get my suitcase,' said Tam cheerfully.

When he had gone, Hamish said severely, 'I'm warning you, Milly. If you find that money, you must tell me immediately. That way you will be safe.'

They heard Tam come back in and dump his suitcase in the hall.

'I'm off,' said Hamish. 'Any sight or sound of anyone, call the police immediately.'

Tam came in as Hamish left.

'Oh, Tam!' cried Milly, tears running down her face. 'I've been so miserable. There's something I've got to tell you.'

He came and sat beside her and took her hands in his. 'What's that?'

Milly dried her tears. She was about to tell him about the money but something stopped her. Tam would no doubt tell her to give it to the police, and he would write a story about it. One thing she knew about Tam: he lived for the next good story.

'I'm a bit shy about . . . well . . . sex. Do you mind waiting? I'm so afraid of Prosser coming back that I feel all cold and frightened.'

'I'll wait, pet, don't worry about it. But you could do with more security. You could do with security lights, front and back. I'll fix it.'

Milly took off Giles's engagement ring and placed it on the table. 'I should throw this away.'

'Sell it,' said the ever-practical Tam.

A week later, on a rare beautiful sunny day, two schoolboys from Drim, Wayne and Dexter Mackay, were playing truant. They had got on to the school bus that morning and waved goodbye to their parents. It was still dark when the bus stopped at an outlying croft to pick up another boy. While the boy's mother was talking to the driver, who had got down from the bus, Wayne and Dexter had crept quietly away, hiding behind a wall until the bus drove off.

In Wayne's bag was half a bottle of sweet sherry he had stolen from his parents' sideboard. As the sun came up, it turned into an unusually mild and still day. Dexter had a collapsible fishing rod in his bag. 'We'll gang up tae that tarn. There's said to be a muckle great fish in the water.'

As the sun rose higher in the sky and the air smelled of wild thyme, they scampered up to the tarn. They lay down by the lip, swigged the sherry, and ate the contents of their lunch boxes. Then Dexter assembled his fishing rod.

'Let's lean over and see if we can see thon fish.'

They lay on their stomachs and peered down into the glassy waters of the tarn.

Then they straightened up and looked at each other in alarm. 'There's a car down there,' whispered Dexter, 'and I think there's someone in it. What'll we do?'

'We'll say we got off the bus and went to stretch our legs and he drove off without us,' said Wayne. 'Chuck that sherry bottle. No, dinnae chuck it in the tarn. Pit it in the heather on the road back.'

* * *

Milly had gone for a walk down to the village with Tam. When they returned, they saw police cars outside the house. The press were just arriving.

'Maybe Prosser has been caught,' said Tam.

Blair was waiting for them. He glared at Tam. 'You, get lost. No reporters.'

Milly took Tam's arm. 'Mr Tamworth is my fiancé and he's not going anywhere.'

Blair's piggy eyes gleamed. Here was a woman who had lost one husband and one fiancé and now she was engaged to 'the pig'. Hamish Macbeth had Prosser on the brain. Blair was out to prove that Milly had something to do with both murders.

Hamish arrived but was told by a policeman on guard that Blair had given instructions that he was to wait outside the house. Tam came out and drew him aside.

'Hamish, he's making Milly cry. He's all but accusing her of the murders.'

Hamish phoned the Tommel Castle Hotel and asked if Priscilla was by any chance making one of her rare visits. When her cool voice came on the phone, he told her what was happening and then asked, 'Could you get on to Daviot and complain? He's such a snob, say jump and he'll ask "how high?"'

'All right,' said Priscilla. 'After I phone, I'll come over and claim Milly as a friend. Let's hope she plays along.'

236

Hamish waited. He wondered why Priscilla had not been in touch with him. Maybe she had only just arrived.

Milly was in the depths of despair. The car had been lifted out of the tarn and the decomposing body of Giles Brandon had been found. Blair was bullying and threatening and the questions went on and on. Then the door opened and a beautiful vision walked in. 'Mr Blair,' said Priscilla, 'I have a message from Superintendent Daviot. You're to phone him right away.'

Blair glared at her but stomped out of the room. Priscilla bent over Milly. 'We're dear friends, right?'

Milly gave a startled nod.

'We'll just wait until he goes away and then I'll make you some tea.'

Milly waited anxiously. Then they heard cars driving off. Jimmy Anderson came in with a grin on his foxy face. 'We're off, Mrs Davenport. Hamish is to take over the questioning.'

'Let's get that tea,' said Priscilla.

In the kitchen, Hamish carefully took Milly over the events of the day when Giles had disappeared. There was nothing new. He'd gone off to Lochdubh and had never returned.

Priscilla had been introduced to Milly. Milly covertly studied her, remembering from village gossip that she had once been engaged to Hamish.

When Hamish put away his notebook, Milly asked plaintively, 'But why Giles? Prosser never knew him, I'll swear.'

'Prosser wants you on your own so he can search for the money. I warn you again that if you find it, you must phone me right away and get Tam here to write a story about it.'

There was a knock at the door. 'That'll be my photographer,' said Tam.

'You mean you're going to write a story?' asked Milly.

'Look, dear, I'm a reporter and I can't sit on this when all the press'll be around soon. Just a picture of you and then I'll write it up. I'll keep the rest o' the press away from you.'

'Good idea,' said Hamish. 'I hope you've got enough groceries in because you'll be under siege for the rest of the day.'

Hamish and Priscilla went outside. 'Thanks,' said Hamish. 'The least I can do is buy you dinner tonight.'

'The Italian? Eight o'clock?'

'Grand.'

Ignoring the reporters, they climbed into their respective vehicles and drove off.

* * *

Back at the police station, Hamish began to worry again about his dog and cat. He had a feeling that Prosser was still going to come after him. Sonsie and Lugs were greedy, and if anyone left out poisoned meat for them, he was sure they would gobble it down. But he couldn't keep moving them out, as some time had now passed and he didn't know when any attack might come.

He put them in the Land Rover and then drove up round the outlying crofts, asking if any stranger had been seen, but no one had spotted anything. Every guest at the hotel had been thoroughly checked through the police computer.

He returned in the evening, changed into his best suit, and brushed his red hair until it shone. Leaving the dog and cat behind, he walked along to the restaurant, wondering why he should feel so excited at the prospect of dinner with Priscilla. Again, he decided it was like the cigarettes he often craved. Addictions never quite went entirely away.

Halfway to the restaurant, he had an uneasy feeling of being watched. He swung round several times but the waterfront was empty.

In the ruins of the hotel that stood by the harbour, Prosser watched him go. He had disguised himself with a moustache and beard and had a false driving licence and passport.

The moment of reckoning had come at last, he thought. He would pick the lock on the police station, shoot those damn animals, and then wait for Macbeth.

Priscilla was as cool and elegant as ever. She was wearing a smoky-blue cashmere twinset over fitted dark-blue corduroy trousers and high-heeled black leather boots.

Hamish's pleasure at seeing her was dimmed slightly. He had that old longing to say or do something that would break through that calm veneer. Wasn't it her very lack of any passion whatsoever that had made him break off the engagement?

But she was always interested in his work and it helped him to go over the cases and to speculate if and when Prosser would arrive.

'Surely he's out of the country by now,' said Priscilla. 'It would be madness to come back here.'

'He is mad. Only a psychopath goes around killing people the way he does, and he has all the extreme vanity of the psychopath. Oh, well, I've got a more immediate worry: they've decided to billet another constable on me and I've got to put the stuff back into the spare room.'

Prosser picked the lock on the police-station front door, not knowing it was hardly ever used; Hamish and the villagers used the

240

kitchen door. He pushed and strained and finally got it open. He looked up and down. No one around. He entered the room and fell over several piles of junk on the floor. Hamish had dumped some of the stuff from the spare room on to the living-room floor. Where were these damn animals?

He went into the kitchen and risked switching on the light. Lugs stood glaring at him out of his blue eyes.

'Goodbye, doggy,' said Prosser with a grin and raised his revolver.

Where the cat came from, he did not know. Sonsie flew straight at him. She was a big wild cat and the onslaught knocked him off-balance and he fell backwards on to the floor. He screamed as the cat bit into his neck, right into the carotid artery. He tried to seize the cat but she leapt back. Blood was pumping out of the wound on his neck. He staggered to his feet, looking for his gun, but the dog sank its teeth into his leg. The cat jumped on his back and began clawing at his head.

His eyes grew dim and he fell to the floor, blood pumping from his neck.

Hamish and Priscilla were just finishing their meal when Willie Lamont approached the table, looking worried.

'Sonsie and Lugs are outside and Sonsie's covered in blood.'

Hamish, followed by Priscilla, rushed out of the restaurant. Hamish knelt down by his cat. Sonsie gave a deep throaty purr. 'Get me a sponge and water,' he shouted over his shoulder to Willie, who had followed them out.

When Willie reappeared with a sponge and a bowl of water, Hamish gently sponged the cat's fur and heaved a sigh of relief. 'She's not injured. I'd better get back to the station.'

'Maybe you've got rats,' suggested Willie.

'I'll see,' said Hamish, thinking, *Not with that amount of blood.*

He and Priscilla quickly walked to the police station. Hamish unlocked the door, noticing that the kitchen light was on. 'Stay back,' he said to Priscilla. 'It might be Prosser.'

He went to the henhouse where he had hidden a rifle and brought it out, followed by the startled clucking of his hens.

'Wait here,' said Hamish. He swung open the kitchen door.

A man was lying there in a large pool of blood. Hamish felt for a pulse and found none. He bent down and ripped off the beard and moustache. Prosser.

He went out to Priscilla. 'It's Prosser. He's dead.'

She walked into the kitchen and turned white at the sight that met her eyes.

'Better phone Strathbane,' she said.

'No!' shouted Hamish. 'I can't do that.'

'Why not?'

'Because they'll soon find out my cat killed him and they'll have Sonsie put down.'

'What? For getting rid of a serial murderer?'

'Blair will see to it. Damn. I've got to move this body. He's bound to have a stolen car. I've got to get rid of it as well. I don't want it found near the police station. You guard the body and don't let anyone in.' Hamish went into the office and came back wearing a pair of latex gloves. He gingerly searched in Prosser's pockets until he found a set of car keys.

When he had gone, Priscilla felt she could not bear the sight of the body. She found a travel rug in Hamish's bedroom and threw it over the horrible sight that was Prosser's body.

After what seemed an age, Hamish came back and said, 'There's a vehicle parked behind the old hotel. I'll get rid of it later. He must have bought it, as he had the keys and hadn't hotwired it. I've got to get this body somewhere and dump it. The Land Rover's outside. I've got a couple of pairs of thae forensic overalls. We'll put them on and get the body in the Land Rover.'

Struggling and panting, because Prosser was heavy, they managed to lift the corpse into the back of the Land Rover. Hamish had found Prosser's revolver and had tucked it into one of the dead man's pockets. 'Thanks, Priscilla,' whispered Hamish. 'You can go home now.'

'You'll need a lookout. We may as well go

together. Don't argue. I'm trying very hard not to be sick.'

Hamish put a wheelbarrow in on top of Prosser's body. They both got in, and he drove off under the blazing stars of Sutherland, into the soaring mountains. The sky was clear but there was the faint metallic smell that heralded snow in the air when he finally stopped.

'Now,' he said, 'I'll get the body into the wheelbarrow. Up there's Fraser's Gully. If I tip the body down there, it's a long way down and it'll get smashed on the rocks. With any luck, ferrets and crows and foxes will help to destroy the evidence.'

'Will you ever tell the police?'

'Oh, aye, when I figure the bastard's decomposed enough. You wait here. I can manage this bit on my own.'

He got out and opened the back of the Land Rover. First he took out the wheelbarrow, and then he pulled the body out on to it. Grunting and swearing under his breath, he pushed the wheelbarrow up the steep incline to the edge of the gully.

At the very edge, he tipped the barrow and sent the body flying down. He heard it bouncing off the sharp rocks he knew were down there. Then there was silence.

He dropped Priscilla by her car on the waterfront. She had taken off the forensic suit when they were up by the gully, and he collected it from her.

'Don't you want me to help you clear up the mess?' asked Priscilla.

'You've done enough. Go home.'

When Priscilla walked into the hotel, the night porter exclaimed, 'Why, Miss Halburton-Smythe! You're as white as a sheet.'

'I think I've a touch of flu,' mumbled Priscilla. She fled to the safety of her room, where she was violently sick. *Thank God I never married him*, she thought. *I'm not cut out to be a policeman's wife*.

Sutherland is near the Gulf Stream and so can enjoy some unusually warm days in winter. Hamish blessed the mild days, which would help with the decomposing of the body, and cursed the frosts. He had found Prosser's car and driven it to Inverness airport, where he left it in the car park.

Priscilla had left again without saying good-bye. He thought sadly that after all they had been through on that dreadful evening, she might at least have called to see how he was. He felt guilty because he could sense the ongoing tension in the village and he longed to tell them their worries were over.

But by the end of February, two hill walkers, peering down into the gully, saw the remains of Prosser and called the police. The body had been attacked by crows, eagles, buzzards, and foxes. There was little left but a skeleton and torn clothes.

The couple had phoned Strathbane so it was not until the evening of their discovery that Jimmy Anderson arrived at the station with the news.

'Is it Prosser?' asked Hamish.

'Looks like it.'

'They won't have had any time to check his dental records.'

'Aye, but inside the lining of his coat, we found his real passport and a Cayman Islands bank book. Guildford police have found his dentist and they're sending up the records. He had a revolver as well, and we're checking to see if it was used to kill Brandon – the sweep had his neck broken, Davenport had his head smashed, same with Betty Close. Brandon is the only one who was shot. They think Philomena was drugged and that's why she lost control of the car. Anyway, according to our singing canaries in captivity, Castle and Sanders, they knew he was out to get Davenport. That's why they set up the alibi for him. They said he got Stefan Loncar to put on a mask that evening so that people would think it was him. You remember, it was a Saturday and they swore they'd all been together most of the day.'

'I wonder why Stefan didn't tell me he had stood in for Prosser that evening at the restaurant. Did they never check where they all were the day afterwards?' asked Hamish. 'If Prosser hadn't been seen on the Sunday, we might have guessed he was still up north.'

'They originally thought they were dealing with four very respectable businessmen, members of the Rotary and the Freemasons.'

'Poor Stefan. I wonder what Prosser did with the body.'

'Maybe he just paid him to leave the country by some other route.'

'I'd like to think so,' said Hamish, 'but I doubt it.'

The next morning, Blair phoned Hamish. 'We've found Prosser doon a gully up frae Drim.'

'How long had he been there?' asked Hamish innocently.

'Months, they think. The Highland beasties have made such a meal o' the corpse that there's little left to tell the pathologist how he died. He probably tripped and fell in the dark. A lot of the bones the foxes hadn't gnawed were broken. Anyway, his dentist has been quick off the mark. It's him, all right, so get ower tae Drim and tell the woman she's safe.'

Hamish drove to Drim. He was glad for Milly's sake. Now she would be able to marry Tam.

'I'm so glad,' said Milly when he gave her the news. 'I've been living in fear.'

'Where's Tam?'

'He's down at police headquarters following up the story. Then he's writing up all the background on my husband. He'll be away all day.'

'Are you all right here on your own? Do you want me to call Ailsa or Edie?'

'No, I'd like to sit here for a bit and be quiet.'

'Well, send me an invitation to the wedding.'

'What wed— Oh, that. I'll let you know.'

Castle and Sanders and their wives were brought to Scotland to the High Court in Edinburgh for trial. It went on for three months. They were charged with being accessories to the murder of Henry Davenport. But here, the prosecution came up against difficulties. They all swore they did not know that Prosser had meant to kill Davenport. They said he had been furious because Davenport had told them about a gold mine in Perthshire and had geological proofs to persuade them to put money into it. But there was no actual forensic proof that Prosser had killed Davenport, or, for that matter, the sweep. John Dean, the man who lived in the flat in the Canongate, was taken out of prison where he was serving time for running brothels in Edinburgh but he said he did not know

248

Prosser had killed the prostitute, nor about any other murders.

The jury – or panel as it is called in Scotland – of fifteen was out for three weeks. They eventually came back with a verdict of not proven, a particularly Scottish verdict that means, we think you did it, we can't prove it, don't do it again.

But the jubilant four on leaving the court were arrested again and taken south to await trial for using forged passports, aiding and abetting a murderer, and every other charge the police could think to throw at them.

Hamish had attended the trial but he was not called to give evidence. He had lunch before he left at the Merlin Club with his friend David Harrison. 'I'm right glad he's dead,' said David. 'After you said he might come after me, I've barely slept.'

Hamish thought guiltily of the people he had kept waiting in fear, and all to protect his cat.

Epilogue

Everything has an end.
– Proverb

Lochdubh returned to its usual torpor. It was as if nothing terrible had ever happened. It had taken Hamish a long time to relax. Sometimes he watched real-life television forensic programmes and in one, the killer was identified by one of his own cat's hairs. He had nightmares of them finding one of Sonsie's hairs on the clothes of the dead man and identifying it as belonging to a wild cat; Blair would then make sure the police station was under scrutiny.

He had scrubbed the floor and the walls with bleach but he knew that luminol would betray the scrubbing and might even find a spot of blood he had missed.

But as ordinary lazy day followed ordinary day, he began to relax. He called on Milly one day and found her weeding in the garden. 'I'm going to have a bed of roses here,' she said.

'Aye, well you'd better get a hedge to protect them because the wind could destroy
them. Where's Tam?'

'Working.'

'When's the wedding?'

Milly stabbed the trowel into the earth. 'We
haven't decided yet.'

A car drove up in front of the house and a
tall woman got out. 'Oh, that's my therapist,'
said Milly.

'I didn't know they made house calls.'

'We've become friends and she likes getting
out of Strathbane. I met her through Victim
Support.'

'I'll be off, then. Let me know when the
happy day's going to be.'

That evening, Tam appeared and said, 'I
thought it would be nice if we went to that
new restaurant down in Strathbane.'

'Must we?' said Milly. 'I've got a nice lamb
casserole in the oven.'

'Put it in the fridge. We'll have it tomorrow.'

'All right. I'll just get my coat.'

'Hey, where's that pretty blue dress I bought
you? Put it on.'

Milly went up to her bedroom and pulled
the dress out of the wardrobe. She hated it. She
felt the neck was too low and the skirt was too
short. She sat down on the bed and stared
bleakly into space. She had been married in

her late teens. She had never really lived alone. Recently, Tam had been away a lot on stories. Milly had loved the peace of having days to herself. She glared at the dress. Henry had always told her what to wear. She had given all her clothes away to the Salvation Army and had bought herself comfortable clothes that she wanted.

Her therapist, Christina Balfour, had told her to start being her own woman, but, reflected Milly, after a lifetime of taking orders, it was hard to know where to start.

She slowly put the dress back in the wardrobe and took out one in simple black wool that she had chosen for herself. She put it on along with low-heeled, patent-leather pumps and a thin string of pearls. Then she picked up a bottle of pink nail varnish from the dressing table, opened it, and dribbled some of it down the front of the dress Tam had chosen for her before going downstairs.

'Where's my dress?' asked Tam. 'You look as if you're going to a funeral.'

'I'm so sorry. I spilled nail varnish on it.'

'Never mind. I'll get you something else. Time you smartened yourself up.'

Journalists of Tam's breed talk shop . . . endlessly. It had happened shortly after they became re-engaged. When they were out for an evening, he drank far too much and told

253

endless reporting stories, unaware that it was a monologue and that Milly was sitting quietly on the other side of the table.

He also had begun to expect Milly to only drink one glass of wine so that she could drive him back.

She looked at him sadly. What had happened to the diffident, affectionate Tam? He had never drunk this much before in her company. Towards the end of the meal, his mobile phone rang. He answered it and then said, 'I'm sorry, Milly. Big story. A raid down at the docks. Can you drop me back at the office and I'll get a photographer to drive me.'

Milly paid the bill. That was another thing that had gone wrong. Tam had begun to leave the paying of bills in restaurants to her.

The raid turned out to be a false alarm, so Tam and the photographer dropped in at a pub that was open twenty-four hours for a drinking session.

Tam had been elevated to chief reporter because of his coverage of the Prosser case.

'When's the wedding?' asked the photographer.

'Don't know,' said Tam. 'You know, I'm wondering if I'm daein' the right thing.'

'Och, everyone knows you're daft about the woman.'

'She doesnae seem to 'preciate that I'm a

hot-shot reporter. She pretends to listen but she aye looks as if she's thinking o' something else. What dae ye think o' Kylie Ross?'

'The newsroom secretary? Come on, laddie. She's in her twenties and a knockout. She wouldnae look at you.'

'Thash where you're wrong, buddy. She gave me that look the ither day.'

'What look?'

'Sort of come hisher.'

'Come hither? Tam, you've had enough. I'll take you home.'

'Take me to ma flat.'

Milly had phoned Christina Balfour as soon as she had got back to Drim. 'I can't go through with this marriage,' she wailed.

'Then you must tell him,' said Christina. 'You can't go on being a rabbit.'

'What did you just say?'

'I should not have said that,' said Christina hurriedly. 'But if you are going to have your freedom, you must take a stand. I'll see you tomorrow.'

Milly took a deep breath. 'I don't think I need any more therapy. Thank you and good night.' She hung up. The phone rang a few moments later but she pulled the connection out of the wall.

She opened the front door and looked down towards the village. It was a Saturday night, and a ceilidh was on in the village hall. Ailsa and the others would be there. She put on her coat. She had not seen much of the village women of late, because they always asked her excitedly about the wedding.

The music had fallen silent and one of the villagers was reciting a long poem. Ailsa saw Milly standing in the doorway and hurried to meet her.

'Come and join the fun,' she said. 'Where's Tam?'

'Step outside,' said Milly. 'I need your advice.'

The next day, Tam awoke with a blinding hangover. He took two Alka-Seltzer, struggled into his clothes, swallowed a glass of whisky, and then made his way to the office.

Kylie the secretary smiled at him. She was a pretty Highland beauty with dark hair and creamy skin. Fuelled by that glass of whisky, which had topped up his intake from the night before, Tam said, 'How's about you and me stepping out one evening?'

Kylie smiled patiently. 'I have a boyfriend, Tam.'

Tam stumped off. The photographer from the night before had watched his approach to Kylie. 'How did you get on?' he asked.

Tam shrugged and gave the time-immemorial reply of the rejected reporter. 'Ach, I think thon one's a lesbian.'

* * *

Ailsa and Milly were at that moment in the police station in Lochdubh facing a bewildered Hamish Macbeth.

'You want me to tell Tam the wedding's off?' exclaimed Hamish.

'Well, haven't you heard o' community policing?' demanded Ailsa. 'It's your duty.'

Hamish stared at them. Then he took out his notebook and wrote down, 'Tam, it's Milly. I don't want to marry you and I'm going to pack up your stuff and leave it outside the door. We're not suited. I am very sorry but I don't want to see you again.'

Hamish handed Milly his mobile phone and the piece of paper. 'Phone Tam and tell him that,' he ordered.

'I can't!' wailed Milly.

'I'll do it,' said Ailsa.

'Nobody's going to do anything except Milly. Go on, Milly. Soften it down a bit if you must. Here!' He poured her a large glass of whisky. 'Get that down ye.'

'What about me?' demanded Ailsa.

'You'll get your dram if your friend here stiffens her spine and makes that call.'

Milly gulped down the whisky.

She slowly took the phone from Hamish. 'Do you mind leaving me?'

'Leave yourself,' said Hamish callously. 'It's my home. Step outside the door.'

The cat, sensing Milly's fear, gave a low warning hiss. 'You shouldnae have a wild cat,' said Ailsa. 'That beast'll attack someone someday.'

'Mind your own business!' shouted Hamish, and Ailsa stared at the normally mild police sergeant in amazement.

They could hear Milly's quiet voice as she stood outside the kitchen door, but they could not hear what she was saying.

At last she came in. 'It's finished.'

'How did he take it?' asked Ailsa.

'Very well. He said he was made for a better woman. He said he had been going to break it off anyway. I won't leave his stuff outside the door. That's rude. I'll need to face him.'

'Good for you,' said Hamish. 'You've got your independence at last.'

'How's Angela Brodie?' asked Ailsa.

'Just fine,' said Hamish. 'She had a taste o' fame and didn't like it one bit.'

But Angela at that moment had just arrived in Inverness for the Highland Literary Festival to be held in the Dancing Scotsman Hotel. She felt this was one opportunity she could not let go by because she was to be interviewed by Malvin Clegg, the literary critic at the BBC. She'd had her wispy hair permed, but it had turned out frizzy. Her new dress was bright red which, when she tried it on, had seemed to drain colour from her face, so she had applied make-up with an inexpert hand.

But wishful thinking and her bedroom mirror, which was in a dark corner, had persuaded her that she looked sophisticated and much younger.

A platform had been set up in a conference room of the hotel along with seating for a hundred people. As the television cameras were going to film the event, all the seats were taken. There was a green room set aside for authors. Angela had hoped to meet Malvin there and get an idea of what questions he was going to ask but was told she would meet him for the first time on the platform.

She walked on to the platform to a spattering of applause. Malvin appeared from the other end of the platform to enthusiastic applause and sat down facing her. He was a small thickset man with a fake-bake tan and dyed black hair.

The master of ceremonies was the hotel manager, dressed in kilt and full regalia. He made a long speech, boasting about the beauty of the hotel and how the literary festival had been his inspiration. He had a high reedy voice and a thin body. A kilt is a very heavy item of dress and his began to slide south, showing a glimpse of white underpants decorated with naked ladies. The audience began to giggle and he hoisted the kilt up again and then decided to leave the stage after a hurried introduction of Malvin and Angela.

Malvin was in a bad mood. Why had he

agreed to attend this hick festival? He had read Angela's book and found it very sexy, and had hopes of a fling with the author but that had died the minute he set eyes on her.

He began with his first question. 'Do you think you are writing literature?'

'I just write what I can,' said Angela.

'I'll just read out this scene from your book where the heroine is in bed with the local bobby.' He made it sound salacious, and Angela squirmed.

'Now, what we all want to know,' said Malvin, leering at the audience, 'is how you did your research.'

'It is all a product of my imagination.'

'But all fiction is autobiographical in some way.'

'Not in this case,' said Angela.

'Let me read another extract.'

Angela cracked. She had seen her appearance in a mirror in the green room but it had been too late to do anything about it. She got to her feet.

'It is my opinion that you are nothing more than a dirty old man,' announced Angela, and she walked from the stage.

She ran out of the hotel to the car park and drove off. Never again, she thought, will I have anything to do with publicity. But on the road home her mobile rang. She stopped in a lay-by and answered it. Her husband's frantic voice sounded down the line. 'What have you been up to? The press are hammering at the door saying you called Malvin Clegg a dirty old man.'

'I'll hide out somewhere,' said Angela.

'What about me? And they won't go away unless you give them something, even if it's no comment.'

'I'll come home,' said Angela wearily.

The aborted interview was shown on all the TV news stations. Malvin could not sue Angela because she had said that it was her opinion. In Edinburgh, her publisher rubbed his hands in glee and went off to order a large reprint.

Angela, with a scarf tied over her frizzy hair and her make-up scrubbed off, faced the press on her doorstep. 'I am sorry,' she said. 'I have nothing to say.'

Hamish Macbeth cleared a path for her through the shouting reporters, and she thankfully escaped inside her house.

Afterwards, Hamish wished he had let her fight her own way into her house as his photo appeared in some newspapers along with descriptions of Angela's heroine having an affair with the village policeman.

When Tam arrived that evening to pick up his belongings, Ailsa was there with Jock Kennedy and several other men from the village. He asked to speak to Milly but was told she was resting and to take his stuff and leave. As he drove away, Tam began to wonder if he'd not gone a little mad. He and Milly had enjoyed something special and he had ruined it. He wondered if he had subconsciously destroyed it because he had always avoided commitment. And why had he started to drink so much when he took her out for an evening?

He shook his head sadly. At least there was always work to take his mind off her.

By dint of thieving passports, Sandra Prosser had made her way to Jensen Beach in Florida. She rented a small flat in a condominium full of old people. After a week, she was bored. The money would not last for ever. She did not have the courage to try to open a bank account and get money transferred from the Cayman Islands but also because she had a shrewd suspicion that her husband would have cleared out that account. She hired a car and drove down into the pretty town of Stuart, looking at the shops, and wondering for the first time if it would not be easier to just give herself up.

She missed her husband. She had not cried when she had learned of his death, but now she remembered the good times they had enjoyed, the expensive trips abroad, and the generous allowance he had given her.

Sandra went into a bar, sat up on a bar stool, and ordered a vodka and tonic. 'How much?' she asked the barman.

'The gentleman over there wishes to pay for it.'

Sandra swung round. A man dressed in expensively casual clothes raised his glass to her. Sandra picked up her own glass and went to join him.

'I'm Vic Faziola,' he said. 'You're new here, aren't you?'

'Visiting for a bit,' said Sandra. He was about her own age with thick brown hair greying at the temples. He had a sallow face and small black eyes. 'What does one do around here?'

'People go swimming or surfing. I own this tavern so it keeps me busy. You English?'

'Yes.'

'What brings you to Florida?'

'Just a holiday. I thought some sun would be nice.'

'Why don't you meet me here at eight this evening and I'll take you for dinner. I like getting to know the visitors.'

Sandra went back to her flat, feeling happy. It was nice to know she still had pulling power. But the afternoon stretched out ahead. She decided to go swimming and then find a hairdresser.

She put her swimsuit on under a blouse and jeans, stuffed underwear into a bag, drove back to Stuart, and headed for the beach.

Great glassy waves curled on to the shore. The sun beat down. It was very hot. Sandra had left her wallet and the bag with the dwindling money in her flat.

She left her clothes on the beach and plunged into the water. She was a powerful swimmer. With steady strokes, she headed out to sea and then turned on her back and floated, dreaming that her new companion would turn out to be her escape from looming poverty.

A log floated past and scraped her arm. Sandra cursed and decided to head for shore. She turned on her front. As she raised her head, she saw the figure of a lifeguard shouting something through a loudhailer, but the wind had risen and she could not hear what he was saying. Probably a storm coming. She raised her head again. Now he was running towards the water, pointing frantically.

Maybe a boat was coming up on her. She twisted her head around and that's when she saw it – a dorsal fin cutting through the waves in her direction. Sandra began to swim as hard as she could. But she was too late.

Great teeth plunged into her leg. She let out a scream of pure terror. Then she disappeared under the waves and a red stain spread out over the blue water.

* * *

It took a long time to recover the bits of Sandra from the sea and put them together with a woman who was missing from the condominium. Her flat was searched and several stolen passports recovered. It was unclear how she had managed to pass through passport controls at airports, where she would get fingerprint and retina scrutiny. But Sandra had driven to Mexico, picking out-of-the-way border controls, and once she was in Mexico had bribed a trucker to take her across the border into the States.

From fingerprints found in her flat, Interpol identified her at last as the missing Sandra Prosser.

Hamish Macbeth had to read about it in the newspapers, angry that neither Jimmy nor anyone at Strathbane had taken the trouble to tell him. Normally lazy and unambitious, and usually glad of a chance to go fishing, he nonetheless could not shake off his irritation. He finally drove to Strathbane and ran Jimmy to earth in the detective's favourite pub.

'Why didn't you tell me Sandra Prosser had been found?' demanded Hamish.

Jimmy grinned. 'You mean, what was left of her? A fitting end. She lived with a shark and got killed by one.'

'So why didn't you tell me?'

'Stop glaring at me. I've been right busy. I somehow thought you'd hear. Sorry. Have a real drink.'

'I'm driving,' said Hamish huffily.

'Well, now you're here, I'll give you the latest horror story in the Prosser saga. Someone in Jensen Beach took a photo of her. Some woman taking a picture of her child but there's a clear shot o' Sandra in the background. They start backtracking through her travels. Found she had been staying in a hotel in Santiago and had spent the night with a young man called Jaime Gonzales, subsequently reported missing. He worked at a clothing firm. He handed in his notice the day after his fling with our Sandra – who had been trying to find him, and paid a girl at the hotel to interpret for her. Next thing, Jaime's mother reports him missing. As they live in a shanty town, the police don't care much. The interpreter said that Sandra was very angry. I think this Jaime stole money from her. The safe in the villa in Rio had been cleaned out. I think she caught up with him and killed him to get the money back. Of course, she must have been really tough to live with a psycho like Prosser.

'Cheer up, Hamish. It's the final chapter. You can write The End and get back to poaching.'

Hamish decided to do just that. When he returned to the police station, he collected his rod and fishing tackle and, with the dog and cat at his heels, walked up over the moors until he came to the upper reaches of the River Anstey.

Keeping a careful eye out for the water bailiff, because the fishing rights belonged to Colonel Halburton-Smythe, he cast his fly on a glassy pool and felt, for the first time in ages, all the dark worry of the Prosser case fade away.

He broke off for a picnic lunch and had just opened a thermos flask when Sonsie gave a warning hiss but Lugs wagged his tail.

Hamish stood up and saw Elspeth Grant coming down the heathery slope towards him.

'You gave me a fright,' he said. 'I thought you were the water bailiff. How did you find me?'

'Elementary, my dear Watson. It's a fine day, the murders are over, and I remembered this was your favourite poaching site.'

They sat down together on a flat rock by the pool. 'Coffee?' asked Hamish.

'Fine. Just black.'

'You look like your old self,' said Hamish. Elspeth's hair was frizzy, and she was wearing an old sweater over a pair of jeans. 'What brings you?'

'Just a holiday.'

'I would have thought they would have sent you back up on the Prosser case.'

'I didn't want to risk anyone pinching my job as a news presenter so I got a new contract stating that that was my sole job. So, in future, everyone can murder everyone up here and you won't see me. Tell me all about it.'

'Too fine a day,' said Hamish. 'I want to forget it.'

Elspeth studied him with those silvery gypsy eyes of hers. 'Prosser evidently knew this territory like the back of his hand,' she said. 'Funny him falling down that gully.'

'I don't want to talk about it!' snapped Hamish, and in a milder voice, 'Sandwich? It's chicken.'

'Thanks. It won't be one of your hens, anyway. You just let them die of old age. I'll take you for dinner tonight. Don't stand me up. Eight o'clock?'

'I'll be there. I think maybe I'll pack up. The fish don't seem to be biting. I really ought to go over to Drim and see how Milly Davenport's getting on.'

Milly had never lived in a house with a cesspool before. So when the sink and toilet started backing up, she phoned Ailsa for help. Ailsa gave her the number of a local man who would come and pump out the cesspool.

Three men with a truck with a big tank on the back arrived. 'I mind the drain is somewhere ower here,' said the boss. He approached the flower bed where the money was buried. 'Not there, surely,' shouted Milly.

'No, no, missus. Jist the ither side, covered in the gravel.' He scraped the gravel away and revealed an iron cover. He wrenched and turned and finally pulled the cover off. A fountain of excrement, fuelled by trapped gases, blasted into the air, spraying everyone with the worst kind of filth.

It poured down into the flower bed and Milly thought with dread of the case of money buried underneath.

When the gusher subsided, the boss, seemingly unfazed by the fact that he was covered in brown unmentionable, put the huge hose into the drain and then started a motor in the truck. Milly ran into the house and stripped off her clothes and had a shower. Then she dressed in clean clothes and went outside again.

The smell was awful. Amused villagers had gathered to watch. A cesspool clearance was regarded as a rare show. When the job was pronounced finished, Jock Kennedy and some of the men asked Milly if she had a hose.

'Yes,' said Milly. 'There are some gardening things in a shed at the side there. What are you going to do?'

'We'll chust be washing this muck off the garden.'

Milly thought frantically of the buried money. 'Oh, don't bother . . .' she began, but Jock was already walking to the shed.

He came back with a long coil of hose. Not bothering to ask Milly's permission, he went into the house and fed the hose from the kitchen tap round to the front of the house and began to drench the garden.

Finally Jock stopped and looked up at the black clouds streaming in from the west. 'Storm's coming, Milly,' he said cheerfully. 'That'll finish the job.'

To Milly's dismay, Ailsa, who had joined the watchers, said cheerfully, 'I think we could all do with a cup of tea.'

Milly felt she could not refuse. They would wonder why. Jock, Ailsa, and the villagers gathered in the kitchen. Milly made endless cups of tea and sliced cake. Outside the wind screamed and the rain flooded down.

After two hours, they left. Milly hurriedly donned a raincoat and rain hat and went out into the garden. The screaming gale lifted her hat from her head and sent it sailing off.

She went to the shed and took out a spade and began to dig. The excrement had sunk down into her new flower bed, and the smell was awful. She hoisted out the attaché case and carried it into the kitchen.

She laid it on the table and opened it. The notes inside were brown with the muck from the cesspool and soaking wet.

Milly found a ball of string and began to put lines of string across the kitchen. Then she began to gingerly sponge each note and pin it up to dry. She stoked up the Raeburn stove and returned to the long, long job of cleaning the banknotes.

Hamish Macbeth drove up to Milly's house. He wrinkled his nose at the smell, which had never quite gone away. He knocked at the door. There was no answer, although he could see Milly's car parked at the side of the house. He thought that she must be down in the village. But after so many scares and murders, he wondered if she was all right. He tried the door and found it unlocked.

Milly had heard the knock at the door but decided if she did not answer it, whoever it was would go away.

She was just pinning up a wet note when she sensed a presence behind her and turned round. Hamish Macbeth stood there.

'I see you've found the money,' he said.

'It's my money,' said Milly shrilly.

'Oh, aye? And do you often wash it? I've heard of laundering money but this is the first time I've seen it actually done.'

'It's mine,' said Milly desperately. 'It was my husband's and now it belongs to me.'

Hamish sat down slowly at the kitchen table. He took off his hat. If he put in a report, it would show that Milly had every intention of keeping the money. By the mess of it, it must have been buried in the garden. He had heard over in Lochdubh about the cesspool clearance.

Prosser had been a criminal, and the money should be impounded.

Milly stood before him, tears running down her face. What an irritatingly weak woman, he thought savagely, realizing for the first time how easy it would be to bully her. Blair, for one, would have a field day.

'How much?' he demanded.

'About seven hundred and fifty thousand,' whimpered Milly, 'or it was when I first counted. I've used some of it.'

'And what do you plan to do with it?'

'I can stay on here. Spend it in the village.'

Hamish thought again of Blair and of the paperwork involved.

He stood up. 'I'm off,' he said. 'I neffer saw the damn money. Get it?'

Milly seized his hand. 'Oh, thank you! Thank you!'

Hamish jerked his hand free and walked out of the kitchen.

When Hamish returned to the police station, he found the editor of the *Highland Times* waiting by the kitchen door.

'Now what?' asked Hamish. 'I've had enough of murders and mayhem to last me a lifetime.'

'Nothing like that,' said Matthew. 'It's a bit o' news that might interest you.'

'Come ben to the kitchen and let's hear it.'

Matthew sat down at the table and took out

some notes. 'You remember that Prosser was conned over some gold mine.'

'Yes, it did seem daft. I kept wondering why he was conned.'

'Well, you know the price of gold is now sky-high?'

'Aye, I read about it.'

'You know where Tyndrum lies, over by the mountains that march eastward along Glen Cononish?'

'Yes.'

'It's going to be Scotland's first gold mine. Chris Sangster – he's the chief executive of Scotgold and a mining engineer – says that each ton of rock is likely to yield up to ten grams of high-grade gold, worth around two hundred pounds. It was talked about before in the sixties when the British Geological Society found evidence of gold in the Western Highlands, but the price of gold was so low, nothing was done about it.

'They're all excited over in Tyndrum. I mean Tyndrum is only a straggle of houses along the main road from Perth and Glasgow to Oban and there isn't much employment. Scotgold expects approval from Loch Lomond and the Trossachs Planning Authority by early summer. So the conning captain might have been on to something.'

'Prosser's papers have been checked. The geological survey was a forgery and put the gold over by Ben Nevis,' said Hamish. 'If the

273

captain had stuck to the straight-and-narrow path and invested in Scotgold, he might have made something.'

They sat talking and then Hamish cried, 'Look at the time! I'm late.'

Without changing out of his uniform, he hurried along to the Italian restaurant. The storm had passed, and the night was clear and starry.

'I was about to leave,' said Elspeth coldly. 'You smell awful. In fact, you thought so little about this date, you couldn't even get out of your uniform and take a bath.'

'It's like this,' said Hamish. 'I was over at Milly's and she was getting her cesspool cleaned. Then Matthew called with a story and I forgot the time.'

'You forgot the . . . ?' Elspeth grabbed her handbag and marched out of the restaurant.

Hamish tried to rush after her but fell head first over his cat and dog who were stationed outside. Thanks to the huge cat flap on the kitchen door, they could come and go as they pleased. Hamish cursed as he got to his feet in time to hear Elspeth driving off in her car.

He wearily returned to his police station, wishing he were not such an indulgent owner and could nail that cat flap shut. Instead, he took off his uniform and bagged it up. He put on clean clothes and drove to an all-night laundrette in Strathbane where they had a coin-operated dry-cleaning machine. As he sat and waited, he reflected it was amazing how a smell in the air could permeate his clothes like that.

'Milly's found that missing money,' said Ailsa to her husband two days later.

'Did she tell you?'

'Not her. But smell that. She bought groceries with this twenty-pound note.'

Jock smelled it and wrinkled his nose. 'It smells of perfume and . . .'

'Shite!' said Ailsa. 'The way I see it, she must have had it buried in the garden and all the money got soaked. Look how wrinkled the note is, as if it's been in the water.'

'Are we going to tell anyone?'

'Of course not. She buys all her stuff in our shop. I'll take her money, smelly or not!'

The next day, Hamish felt he should call on Elspeth. He had stood her up so many times that her anger was understandable.

He was about to go to Strathbane and buy a bunch of roses when the post arrived and, with it, his bank statement. He had gone into the red. With the statement came a letter from the bank manager asking him to do something about the overdraft.

He went along to the offices of the *Highland Times*, seized a paper, and looked at the local events. There was the Highland Games at

Braikie in a week's time. It was a big event, sponsored by a building society and a bank. The prize for the hill running event was five thousand pounds.

Hamish drove to Braikie and entered his name. Then he returned to Lochdubh and changed into shorts and T-shirt and began to run up over the moors to the slopes of the mountains.

Elspeth went into Patel's to buy some midge repellent. 'Aye, they're bad the day,' said Mr Patel. 'What's our Hamish up to?'

'I'm sure I don't know,' said Elspeth coldly, and the curiosity overcame her. 'Why?'

Mr Patel grinned. 'The greater red-legged Hamish has been seen running through the village like the wind and then up into the mountains. He must be in training for the hill race at Braikie.'

Elspeth felt low. These days she was a celebrity. The only person who did not want her company seemed to be Hamish Macbeth. Of course, he had turned up at the restaurant but in such a state! And to think how carefully she had dressed.

Luckily for Hamish, there was no crime during the week of arduous training that he put in.

He was expected to police the games so, on

the great day, he put on his uniform, put his running gear in a bag, nailed the cat flap shut because he knew if he took his pets they would try to run with him as they had when he was training, and set out for the games.

It was a fine day with only wisps of cloud across the blue sky. He was alarmed at the number of people who stopped him and said they had put money on him. Willie the gamekeeper was running a book and Hamish was tempted to arrest him for illegal gambling, frightened of all the money people would lose if he did not win, but he had never done such a thing before and decided to turn a blind eye.

At last, it was time for him to change and get to the starting line. As the pistol went off, he set off at an easy pace. Suddenly he did not care if he won or not. He was enjoying the beauty of the day and the exercise.

Up on the slopes of the moors, the Harris brothers rose from the heather and shouted, 'Murderer! We'll see you after the race.'

The night when he had pushed Prosser's body up to the gully flashed into Hamish's mind. If that evil pair had seen anything, then his career was over, not to mention his life in Lochdubh. Fuelled by a spurt of fury and anxious to get the race over with and find out what they knew, he began to run like the wind.

When he approached the finishing line, he was deaf to the cheering crowd. He realized he had won. He looked around for the Harris brothers, but they were nowhere in sight. He changed back into his uniform and began to patrol the games again, stopping here and there to accept congratulations.

At the end of the day, he stood on the platform with the other prizewinners and accepted his cheque and a small silver cup.

As he finally stepped down from the platform, Ian and Pete Harris suddenly appeared in front of him.

'You'll chust cash that cheque on the Monday morning and gie us the cash,' said Ian, baring broken and blackened teeth in a grin.

'Come with me,' said Hamish. He walked quickly outside the field to his Land Rover.

'Now, why should I do that?' he demanded.

'We saw you, that nicht,' said Ian, 'up at Fraser's Gully, pushing thon dead man ower the edge.'

'Aye,' said Pete, 'there didnae seem much point in mentioning it afore because everyone knows you havenae any money.'

Hamish surveyed them, his hazel eyes hard as agate. 'So that's where you keep your still,' he said.

They both looked at him in alarm.

'I've been looking for it. You murmur one word o' this and I'll be up there with a sledge-hammer and I'll smash the damn thing to pieces and then I might take it to you. And who's going to believe you? A couple wi' criminal records or a policeman?'

There came a low, snake-like hiss. Sonsie and Lugs were standing there. Sonsie's eyes were blazing yellow.

'Get the cat away,' shouted Ian. 'It's the devil!'

'Are you going to be good?' asked Hamish.

'Oh, aye, aye, richt enough,' said Ian.

'Chust our wee joke,' said his brother. 'We didnae see anything.'

They hurried off. Hamish looked down at his pets. 'How did you get out?'

'I let them out.' Elspeth appeared from the other side of Hamish's Land Rover. 'They were making a noise, Sonsie howling and Lugs barking like mad. I let myself into the police station. You'd nailed the cat flap shut. They told me you were at the games so I brought them. Now, what were those villains talking about?'

'It's a long story.'

'And it's dinner time,' said Elspeth. 'You can buy me dinner and tell me about it.'

Stefan Loncar sat in a dismal cold room in Sofia in Bulgaria. He had been afraid that Prosser might have been waiting for him at the airport and so he had travelled overland, choosing Sofia as a good place to hide out. He had finally found some old British newspapers and learned of the death of Prosser and the arrest of the others. He was working as a dishwasher in a restaurant during the evenings. His pay was meagre and he could not afford any drugs apart from an occasional bit of cannabis. He sometimes wondered if he would not have been more comfortable in a British prison.

At dinner at the Italian restaurant, Hamish told Elspeth the whole story, knowing he could trust her.

When he had finished, Elspeth asked, with an odd look on her face, 'Doesn't that cat of yours ever frighten you?'

'Sonsie? No. Gentle as anything.'

'Do you believe people come back as animals?'

'That's Highland superstition!'

'I'll tell you one thing, you nearly got married twice and I bet that damn animal from hell knew nothing was going to come of it. If you ever do fall in love, watch out, Hamish Macbeth!'

'You're talking havers.'

'I know a jealous woman when I see one.'

'For heffen's sakes, lassie. It's a cat!'

'We'll see,' said Elspeth. 'We'll see.'

JOIN
M.C. Beaton
ONLINE

www.mcbeaton.com/uk

Keep up with her latest news, views, wit & wisdom
And sign up to the M. C. Beaton newsletter

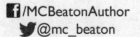
/MCBeatonAuthor
@mc_beaton